Josh gazed lovingly down at Lynne. "What a couple of dummies we are," he murmured, tracing her kiss-swollen mouth with a fingertip. "Those trees sure fooled us."

"What trees?" Lynne asked breathlessly. The feel of Josh's hard body against hers sent rivers within her flooding their banks. She was dizzy with desire.

"The ones we were looking at that made us miss the forest," he whispered. "And nearly made me miss making love to you...."

THE AUTHOR

Mary Jo Territo has lived in New York City for a number of years. She worked in the theater and later as an editor at Richard Gallen Books, before starting to write stories of her own.

Mary Jo enjoys bicycling, running and skiing—all activities that offset the effects of spending long hours at her word processor. This newly married author also writes as Kathryn Belmont and Gwen Fairfax.

Just Friends
MARY JO TERRITO

Harlequin Books

TORONTO • NEW YORK • LONDON
AMSTERDAM • PARIS • SYDNEY • HAMBURG
STOCKHOLM • ATHENS • TOKYO • MILAN

To Miriam—
more than just a friend

Published March 1985

ISBN 0-373-25152-1

Copyright ©1985 by Mary Jo Territo. All rights reserved.
Philippine copyright 1985. Australian copyright 1985.
Except for use in any review, the reproduction or utilization of
this work in whole or in part in any form by any electronic,
mechanical or other means, now known or hereafter invented,
including xerography, photocopying and recording, or in any
information storage or retrieval system, is forbidden without
the permission of the publisher, Harlequin Enterprises Limited,
225 Duncan Mill Road, Don Mills, Ontario, Canada M3B 3K9.

All the characters in this book have no existence outside the
imagination of the author and have no relation whatsoever to
anyone bearing the same name or names. They are not even
distantly inspired by any individual known or unknown to the
author, and all incidents are pure invention.

Reprinted from "True Love" by Cole Porter, copyright © 1955 & 1956
by Chappell & Co., Inc. Copyright Renewed, Assigned to Robert H.
Montgomery, Trustee of the Cole Porter Musical & Literary Property
Trusts. Chappell & Co., Inc., owner of publication and allied rights
throughout the world. International Copyright Secured. All Rights
Reserved. Used by permission.

The Harlequin trademarks, consisting of the words, TEMPTATION,
HARLEQUIN TEMPTATION, HARLEQUIN TEMPTATIONS, and
the portrayal of a Harlequin, are trademarks of Harlequin Enterprises
Limited; the portrayal of a Harlequin is registered in the United
States Patent and Trademark Office and in the Canada Trade
Marks Office.

Printed in Canada

1

WHACK! LYNNE FARRELL SLAMMED the speeding squash ball into the corner of the court and watched it ricochet over her opponent's head. *Get that one,* she thought gleefully, letting her body relax slightly.

Wham! She heard the crack of racket against ball and saw the small black sphere whizzing toward the front wall. Lynne's body tensed instantly. She lunged low and scooped her racket down, but the ball dribbled past her. Panting, Lynne watched it roll to the back of the court.

"Wahoo! All right! You owe me breakfast, Farrell."

Lynne eyed her opponent coolly. "Don't worry. You'll get yours." She started for the back of the court and gathered up her gear. Throwing her towel around her neck she said, "I was too confident this morning. Thought you'd be soft after two weeks of lolling on the beach. What did you do? Run six miles a day?"

"Only five."

"Son of a gun," Lynne exclaimed. "That'll teach me to make assumptions. Nice going."

"Thanks."

"Enjoy it while you can," she warned. "I won't be unprepared next time." The bell rang in the courts, signaling the end of the period. Lynne opened the door. "Meet you downstairs in fifteen minutes. And don't spend all morning gossiping in the locker room," she added with a grin.

"Would I keep a lady waiting?" Josh Simmons mopped his face with his towel and gave Lynne a companionable rap on the arm.

"I don't know. Would you?" Lynne asked lightly.

In the women's locker room Lynne stripped off her sopping shorts and T-shirt, removed the terrycloth sweatbands from her forehead and wrists and headed for the shower. She waited until it was steamy and stepped right under the spray, letting the pulsing jet stream mold her auburn hair to her head. Then she turned so that the soothing water could pommel her neck and shoulder muscles.

The shower felt so luxurious she could have stayed in it forever, but she forced herself to soap down her slim, well-toned body and to lather up a handful of shampoo and wash her hair. She toweled off briskly, blow dried her carefully layered chin-length hair in a matter of minutes and stepped into her favorite fall outfit, a forest-green-and-gray plaid in heavy cotton, the skirt midcalf length and gently full, the matching top loose with long sleeves. Around her waist she tied a wide belt of soft green leather.

Her makeup was quick and easy: a dab of mascara to accentuate her graceful green eyes, a dusting of corn-silk powder to tone down the natural ruddiness of her complexion, a dollop of pale rose gloss spread on her full lips. Lastly, she slipped her feet into gray leather pumps with low heels—as much for comfort as to minimize her above-average height—and picked up her bags.

Just Friends

You might think I was going away for the week, instead of to work for the day, Lynne thought, as she positioned her black leather purse on her left shoulder, hefted her squash bag in her left hand and her briefcase, bulging with manuscripts, in her right.

Lynne looked balefully at the heavy leather case. It was the only thing she didn't like about being an editor. Everything else was terrific. So terrific that sometimes she couldn't believe she was actually paid—although not very much—to sit in a room all day and work with books. Of course there was more to it than that. She had to negotiate contracts, cultivate relationships with agents and authors, and make sure the sales and promotion staff paid proper attention to her projects. It was hectic, downright tense at times, but she thrived on it. Lugging manuscripts back and forth from office to home, however, was a drag. If only she could train them to transport themselves from one place to another. Maybe she'd have a word with the science-fiction editor....

By means of the elevator, Lynne transported herself down to the lobby of the squash club. As she stepped out of the car, balancing her load, Josh rushed forward.

"Let me give you a hand." Before she could protest, he reached for her briefcase. His hand grazed hers as he took it from her. "Holy cow," he said, as he hefted the heavy case. "Now I know why you *used* to beat me at squash."

"You don't have to rub it in," she replied lightly, fighting the flush she felt creeping into her cheeks. "And why so gallant this morning?" He didn't usually offer to carry her manuscripts. After all, they were just friends.

"I don't know. I saw you with all that...and I just...." A momentary look of confusion shadowed his usually sparkling black eyes. "Would you rather I didn't?"

"No, of course not," Lynne responded hastily to his slightly wounded tone. For a moment she was taken aback. For reassurance she looked at Josh, at the square-jawed face now tanned to a toasty bronze, the curly dark hair neatly parted in defiance of its natural inclination, the fine straight nose, the jutting chin, the honest mouth. It was the same as always, but.... It was only because she hadn't seen him in two weeks that he looked so handsome, she told herself. "I was just a little surprised." To assure herself as much as Josh she added, "That's all. Look, I'm starving. Are we going to stand here jabbering all morning, or am I going to buy you breakfast?"

"Breakfast it is."

"How many is this now? Three?" Lynne asked as they left the club and walked downtown on Lexington Avenue. She thought back to the day she'd run into Josh in the lobby of the squash club. They'd known each other slightly in college but hadn't seen each other since. Lynne, who had been captain of her college team and a nationally ranked competitor, had lost her regular squash partner. Josh had just joined the club and had never played more than casually. She was skeptical when he'd proposed the arrangement, but Josh's eagerness and greater strength had evened the odds somewhat. Though he'd improved rapidly, she beat him soundly and regularly until June, when he won his first victory. Lynne had bought him breakfast that morning at the Apollo Coffee Shop near Seventy-fourth Street. They'd been having breakfast there—Dutch treat—after their twice-weekly squash games for almost a year. To give herself added incentive she promised to treat him every time he won.

"Four," Josh said emphatically.

"Four?"

"Four. Gorgeous day, isn't it?"

For you maybe, she was tempted to say. But it was so beautiful outside that winning or losing a squash game became an irrelevant petty detail. The air was crisp and clean; a week of cool weather had washed away the last of the heavy haze that hung over the city at the end of the summer. The sky was a clear blue canopy; the sun bright and friendly, not the merciless monster it had been ten days earlier.

"Mmm. I'm so glad the summer's over. One more hot day and I would have melted. It's lovely to be outside and not want to go rushing into an air-conditioned building."

"Say, why don't we have breakfast outside? Go over to Central Park? The sailing pond is just a few blocks from here."

It was the first time that either of them had suggested anything other than a coffee-shop breakfast. But the morning had already been different than most they'd spent together—Josh winning, then carrying her briefcase, now this. "Why not?" she answered. She might as well go with the flow, she thought to herself, taking a deep breath of the fresh invigorating air.

As they walked into the Apollo they were greeted by Rose, who sat at the cash register and handled the takeout orders. She was a pleasant talkative woman, the wife of the owner, dark with a full face. More often than not an open paperback romance lay spine up next to the cash register. Between customers she snuck in a few pages of the story. "Good morning," she said warmly, looking up from her book. "I think Tony has a booth for you in the back."

"Thanks, Rose," Josh replied, "but we're going to take something out this morning."

"Late today?"

"No," he told her. "We're having a picnic breakfast in the park."

"Oooh," Rose cooed. "How romantic. Just like the people in my books."

"Not exactly," Lynne answered, giving Josh a sideways look. Josh just raised his eyebrows slightly. He was clearly enjoying Rose's misconception.

"Well...." he hedged.

"That's what's wrong with you young women," she admonished Lynne. "You've got to keep your romance alive. That's what I'm always telling my Tony. It works, you know. We're together twenty-seven years this November." She beamed with satisfaction. "Now what can I get you folks for your picnic? How about scrambled eggs and bacon on a nice hard roll, juice and coffee. Maybe a Danish?"

"Okay, but just one Danish," Lynne said.

Rose shook her head. "Like a string bean and worried about her weight." She leaned over to Josh. "Why don't you just tell her there'll be more of her to love? That's what my Tony always tells me."

Josh put his elbow on the counter and said in a stage whisper to Rose, "She's a hard woman that way, Rose. Make it one Danish each. Cherry if you've got them."

Rose called in their order to the kitchen and

Lynne and Josh stepped aside so that she could wait on other customers. "I guess Rose thinks we're an old married couple," Josh said with amusement.

"It's not surprising. We've been having breakfast here twice a week for a year. I suppose she didn't notice that you're tanned and I'm not."

Josh grinned. "Separate vacations probably aren't her idea of romance."

"Okay, you two," Rose sang out. "I had them pack your order extra carefully so it won't get cold on the way to the park."

"Thanks a lot, Rose," Lynne said, pulling a bill out of her wallet.

"You two have a good time now. But next time, honey," she whispered to Lynne, "let him pay. It's better that way."

Lynne could hardly keep a straight face as she and Josh left the coffee shop. "If she only knew," she said with a chuckle.

"Let's not tell her. I think she'd be really disappointed."

They walked quickly to the park and down the path that led to the sailing pond. On weekends children of all ages sailed miniature boats on the shallow rectangular pool. Some were elaborate handmade creations, painstakingly modeled after their life-size sisters, others were more-modest craft of molded plastic. There were no sailors out this morning, but many people were walking through the park on their way to work. Some, like Josh and Lynne, were breakfasting alfresco from brown-paper sacks, newspapers folded on their laps or spread out beside them.

They found an empty bench facing the pond and unpacked their food. Josh toasted Lynne with his plastic container of orange juice. "To many more squash games and breakfasts—no matter who wins."

"Or who buys breakfast." Lynne touched her container to his and they both drank thirstily.

"It's good to see you," Josh said. "I didn't realize until this morning that.... Well, I missed you."

"You didn't have to sound that surprised, Josh." She had missed him, too, especially his touching directness. So many of the men she had dated in the past couple of years never said anything, especially where feelings were involved, without tap dancing around the issue. She'd seen a lot of fancy footwork lately. But Josh was not afraid to talk about his feelings. It was one of the many things besides his intelligence and sense of humor that she liked about him. "I missed you, too."

"You did?"

"Of course I did. You're one of my best friends. I missed talking to you. And I missed beating you at squash."

"If I have anything to do with it, you'll still miss that."

Lynne just made a face and bit into her crusty roll. The bacon was tangy and tasty, the eggs soft and fluffy. "Good," she declared. Josh gave her a questioning look. "I meant the sandwich, wise guy."

"Sure," Josh said, taking a bite of his roll.

"Tell me about the beach," Lynne said when she'd taken the edge off her hunger.

"It was great during the week when no one was around. I went out running, took long walks, read a lot, but the weekends were pretty much the same as they've been all summer. I can't believe those guys. Sometimes I think I'm on the set of *Return to Animal*

House. Well," he relented, "it's not quite that bad, but it is a lot like living in a dorm again. I know, I know. You told me so."

"I wasn't going to say anything." But it was true. Against her advice Josh had taken a summer share in a house in Bridgehampton with a group of men he hadn't known beforehand. Rentals at the Long Island beach resort were prohibitively high, and it was common practice for a group of people to get together and split expenses. The principle was fine, but she'd thought it folly to agree to spend every weekend of the summer with strangers. Especially as there would be six men plus guests in the rambling house.

"I don't know how these guys do it. Work hard all week, party hard all weekend. Come Friday night, I'm up for a little peace and quiet, not disco dancing and lapping up a keg of beer. And none of the women around seem interested in anything less hectic. Maybe I haven't met the right ones. Or maybe I'm just getting old."

"You'll be all of thirty-three in January, Josh. Remind me to get you a cane for your birthday."

"Forget the cane. Just find me a good woman."

"What happened to the dancer? I thought she was going to spend some time with you at the beach."

"She was—until she danced herself into someone else's arms."

"I'm sorry," Lynne said.

"All's fair," Josh answered with a shrug, but his averted eyes told Lynne the hurt was deeper than he let on. "Don't you have any friends who are dying to meet a straight, sane, single, solvent financial analyst?"

Lynne polished off the last of her sandwich. "The offer still stands to fix you up with my friend Jenny Howard, the one who teaches at New York University's business school. I think you two would have a lot in common."

"I don't know," Josh said doubtfully. "I hate blind dates."

"Who doesn't?" Lynne took a sip of her coffee, thinking. There had to be a better way to get people together. "You know," she said after a moment, "it doesn't have to be a blind date. The three of us could get together and have a drink somewhere. A perfectly normal human occasion.

Josh shrugged. "Let me think about it. What about you?"

"If you're inquiring about my love life, I can report without doubt that Mr. Right has not come waltzing into my life in the last two weeks."

"I just don't understand it," Josh said with a sigh. "Two perfectly nice people and between us we can't find one good partner. I think we should make a deal. If neither of us meets anyone soon we should marry each other. At least we know we can face each other over breakfast. That's more than a lot of couples can say. Right?"

"You're serious, aren't you?" Lynne asked, looking at him closely.

"Serious enough," he answered. "Wouldn't you like to sail the ship of life with me, Lynnie?" He gestured out over the pond, sparkling gaily in the sunshine, rippling gently in the breeze. Josh drained his coffee and began to tear the container in half.

"Whatever are you doing?"

"You'll see." He took a wooden coffee stirrer from

one of the sacks and an unused paper napkin and began to weave the stick carefully through the napkin. Then he inserted the stick in the container hull. "Want to see if she sails?"

"Sure," Lynne said. "But we have to christen her first."

"How about the *True Love*? Like in that movie with Grace Kelly and Bing Crosby."

"*High Society*," Lynne supplied. "'I give to you and you give to me,'" she sang the first line of the song "True Love" in a light soprano.

"'True love,'" Josh answered in a hearty off-key baritone.

Lynne dipped her finger into her orange-juice container and sprinkled a few drops on Josh's homemade ship. "I christen thee the S.S. *True Love*. May you sail far and wide."

"And bring back precious cargo safely."

They ran down to the pond and knelt at the edge. Josh placed the *True Love* carefully on the water, holding on to the sail until the little boat had stabilized. Lynne held her breath as Josh took his hand off the sail and gave it a gentle push. For a moment the *True Love* floundered, but she righted herself and bobbed off in the direction of the current. Josh leaned back on his heels and threw an arm around Lynne's shoulder. "She's off," he crowed.

His arm felt warm and Lynne let her head drop onto his shoulder. It was great to have friends, to have people who knew you, understood you, cared about you. It smoothed a lot of life's rough edges.

They watched the little boat wobble and bobble its way downstream, swaying in the gentle breeze the way a tanker would sway in a storm. But she stayed upright and pressed on. It looked like she might make it all the way to the nearest corner of the pond. Josh rose and grabbed Lynne's hand. "Come on," he said. "We don't want to miss the docking ceremonies, do we?"

Hand in hand they strolled along the side of the pond, cheering on the *True Love* as she inched along. When the tiny boat was just an arm's length from the corner a sudden gust of wind swept across the pond. The *True Love* began to take on water. Josh reached out to try to rescue her, but the little boat capsized and sank. They knelt at the side, hands still clasped, sadly watching her go down.

The boat had been gone for a few moments before Lynne spoke. "I guess we should both be getting to the office," she said quietly, but made no move to go.

"We can be a few minutes late for once," Josh said. He reached out and touched Lynne's cheek lightly. "I really enjoyed this morning. I wasn't looking forward to coming back to the city, but you made it all right. Thanks."

"Anytime," Lynne replied. "Anytime."

Josh helped her up and they walked slowly back to their bench, cleared up the remains of their breakfast and left the park. For a moment when they reached the street Lynne was a bit disoriented. During their time in the park she had felt she was in a place very far from New York City, but here they were on Fifth Avenue, cars and taxis whizzing past, buses lumbering to a halt at the bus stop. She slipped her free arm through Josh's as they crossed the street.

At Lexington Avenue he waited with her until her

bus came and handed her her briefcase as she was about to board. "I'll see you Friday," he said. "Take care of yourself, Lynne." He leaned over and brushed his lips against her cheek, then hurried off down the street toward the subway.

"Take your time, miss. You're only holdin' up the whole bus. Nobody really wants to get to work. We've got all the time in the world. You wanna give him another kiss? We'll wait." The bus driver gave her a long-suffering smile. Mumbling apologies, Lynne got on the bus and dropped her token in the fare box.

She found a place to stand in front of an elderly woman and reached up to hang on to a strap as the bus lurched into traffic. "You shouldn't let him bother you, darling," the woman said in a thick Yiddish accent. "Everyone in such a hurry. No one going anywhere."

Lynne looked down to murmur something suitably polite to the woman and through the window caught sight of Josh striding jauntily down the street. As her bus passed him, he paused and peered through the dusty windows. Lynne waved and he broke into a broad smile and tipped her a breezy salute. His hair was slightly disheveled from their romp in the park, and under his open suit jacket his tie was askew. He looked happy and bright, like a child at the end of an afternoon's play.

What a nice man, Lynne thought. *What a really nice man.* Funny that they'd never seen each other except on the squash court and for breakfast afterward. But that was New York for you. Lynne bent over to pull her newspaper from her briefcase. So much to do, never enough time. Friends got put into little boxes marked Squash Partner or Person to Go to Galleries With. Maybe it was time to open the boxes and start moving things around.

2

"Great spaghetti, Lynne." Jenny Howard wound another clump of noodles around her fork. "My compliments to the chef."

"A Farrell family favorite for one generation. Garlic bread?" Lynne passed the basket across the table.

"Why not?" Jenny asked, reaching for a piece. "If you're going to pig out, you might as well go all the way." She took a sip of the Chianti Lynne had poured out of a straw-covered bottle. "All we need is some mandolin music and we might think we're in Italy." Lynne had covered her small dining table with a red-checkered cloth and stuck a candle in the neck of an empty wine bottle.

"As long as you don't look out the window and expect a view of the sea or mountains. The music, however, I can supply."

Lynne walked across the room that she had fixed up as a dining-room-cum-library-cum-study in her small railroad flat. It faced an air shaft and the only view was the brick wall of the next building. Aside from that flaw—hidden by bamboo matchstick blinds—the room was comfortable and appealing. The drop-leaf dining table and two mahogany ladder-back chairs sat beside an exposed brick wall beneath the windows. On one of the inside walls Lynne had built floor-to-ceiling wooden bookshelves, which held her stereo equipment. She found a recording of Neapolitan folk music and put it on.

Opposite the bookshelves was her desk, an old mahogany library table that sat on two squat bulbous legs and served as a dining table on those rare occasions when she had more than one or two guests for dinner. In the corner opposite the desk was a comfortable overstuffed rocker with hand-carved arms and petit-point upholstery. Behind it was a reading lamp and beside it an end table overflowing with books and magazines.

"I think you've done wonders with this apartment," Jenny said, "despite its obvious drawbacks."

"Such as a bathroom off the kitchen and having to walk through the bedroom to get to the parlor."

"At least you're not in a boring modern box like mine. Two utterly rectangular rooms and—"

"A view of half of New Jersey. Spare me, Howard." Jenny's high rise at the eastern edge of Greenwich Village watched over the low rooftops of the Village and out over the Hudson and into New Jersey. On a clear day you could see the Watchung Mountains rising gently in the west. "I could do with a little less character and a lot more convenience in this place."

"And storage space. Your bookshelves are filled already, Lynne."

"I know. One of the hazards of working in publishing."

"Or academia. I'm starting to have the same problem."

As they finished their spaghetti and munched on a green salad they talked about their jobs. Lynne had recently been promoted to senior editor at Parker and

Hamilton, a well-respected independent publishing company. Though relatively small in comparison with some of the conglomerate-owned houses, P & H had a wide reputation in the field for integrity as well as innovation. She had begun her career there as an editorial assistant right after college, and had moved up in the house, one of the few people in publishing who hadn't played "musical jobs" to get promotions.

Jenny, after getting her MBA in finance from New York University, had taken a job in banking, then returned to the university to teach first-year MBA students. She was thirty-one, two years older than Lynne, whom she'd met at a party in the Village four or five years earlier.

"We should do this more often," Jenny said. "Cook dinner for each other, I mean. We always end up going out, and usually downtown. I like coming up to the East Side. I hardly ever get above Fourteenth Street anymore. That's what happens when you work around the corner from where you live."

Lynne started to bring the dishes into the kitchen and Jenny rose to help her. "I realized the other day I hadn't had anyone here for dinner since before the summer. I've also been feeling... not exactly in a rut, but that I always do the same things with the same people. I've been trying to mix things up lately. Try some different combinations."

"Do you want to wash these up now or wait?" Jenny asked.

"Now, I think. I didn't make any dessert. Part of my new or different campaign. There's a lovely little bakery-café that opened up a few blocks from here. I thought we could get a cappuccino and a pastry."

"And somebody can roll me back to the Village. I just hope it's all downhill from here."

"Oh, stop it, Jenny. You're not a single ounce overweight." Jenny was slim and delicately built. Her shoulders were narrow, her neck long and thin. She was beautiful, calmly and quietly beautiful, with no trace of flash or brass. Her hair was shoulder length, wavy and golden; the skin that covered her small piquant face was translucent, almost pearllike; her eyes were an opaline blue. One of the joys of knowing Jenny, Lynne had always felt, was the way her angelic looks left you unprepared for her quickness of mind, her strength of character, her lusty laughter.

"And I'd like to keep it that way. But I suppose no one's going to force-feed me a pastry. Shall I dry? I could use the exercise after that meal."

"No, thanks. There isn't enough room in here for two people. Besides, I know how you feel about housework. We don't have to be so proper and polite with each other, do we, Jen?"

Jenny smiled and shook her head. "I'll be in the other room." She sat in Lynne's rocking chair and picked up a magazine, but put it down before even looking at it. She had a nice quiet feeling inside—full and content. The room had a spicy smell, a blend of Lynne's spaghetti sauce and burning candles. Jenny wagged her toe in tempo with the music and set the chair rocking in rhythm.

"Jen?" Lynne called from the kitchen.

"Mmm?"

"I just thought of something. Why don't I call my friend Josh Simmons and ask him to join us? He lives right around the corner."

"The guy you play squash with?"

"Right."

"And the one you offered to fix me up with before I met Andy? If I didn't know that you don't have a devious bone in your body...."

"Honestly, Jenny, I just thought of it. He might not even be home tonight."

"Part of the 'new or different' campaign?"

"Right. And besides, now that you aren't seeing Andy anymore...." Lynne appeared in the kitchen doorway, drying her hands on a dish towel, a cat-eyeing-the-cream smile on her face.

"Why not?" Jenny said gamely.

JOSH SIMMONS LOOSENED HIS TIE and flipped through his mail as the elevator rose slowly to the eleventh floor. His building was an older high rise, the type called prewar in the real-estate advertisements. It was a sturdy brick structure, and if the elevator was not swift and efficient, the rooms in his apartment were more spacious and gracious than those in the newer buildings. The only thing of interest in the stack of paper he'd wrestled out of his small mailbox was a postcard from friends honeymooning in Italy. They certainly sounded happy, he thought enviously.

In his small foyer, Josh deposited his briefcase beside the table and hung up his trench coat in the closet. He dropped mail and keys on the table and went into the kitchen to turn on the oven and stow the cartons of Chinese food he'd picked up on his way from the subway. He didn't bring home food or eat out of cans or in restaurants every evening, like many of his single friends. Most nights at home he cooked himself a simple meal of chicken or fish with a salad, or fresh vegetables. Not that he was a gourmet, but he found a certain satisfaction in preparing his own meals. After sitting at a desk all day reading reports and playing with numbers and abstract concepts, he liked dealing with something concrete like a carrot or a potato. Tonight, though, he wasn't in the mood to cook. What he really wanted was someone at home to cook and eat with him. But there wasn't anyone, and the thought of sitting in a restaurant alone was not appealing. That left the local Chinese takeout shop.

After changing into jeans and a sport shirt he poured himself a beer and flipped on the television news. He spooned up a plate of rice and twice-cooked pork, ripped the paper from the pair of chopsticks that came with the meal and settled himself in front of the TV. He watched the commentator, but his mind was far from what was being reported.

He was thinking about himself, about still being single, never married, never even engaged. It wasn't only the postcard from Italy. In the past couple of weeks—since he'd returned from his vacation at the beach—it seemed that every time the phone rang he got news that another of his friends was getting married or expecting a baby. It was starting to get him down.

He didn't understand it. He wasn't one of those men who didn't want to be married, who thought of matrimony as a fate to be avoided at all costs. He'd always wanted to marry, had never doubted that he would, and thought he'd make a good father. He'd planned on it; even taken it for granted. However, one crucial setback had prevented him carrying out his plan: he'd never found the right woman.

Just Friends

Josh polished off the rest of the Chinese food and leafed through *The New Yorker* to see if there were any good movies playing the neighborhood. He didn't feel like staying home by himself tonight. Usually he enjoyed an evening alone to catch up on reading or to loaf around and listen to music or watch TV. He read every listing, but there was nothing he wanted to see. Maybe he should go to one of the nearby single bars. There were certainly enough of them. But he knew that wasn't what he wanted. They were too noisy, too frenetic, too impersonal. What he wanted was to sit and talk to someone, someone he didn't have to impress or flatter, someone who wasn't sizing up his potential for a "meaningful relationship" any more than he was sizing up hers. Someone he could be comfortable with—like Lynne.

She lived only a few blocks away, but he'd never been to her apartment or she to his. It suddenly struck him as odd that they didn't see more of each other. She'd be just the sort of person to have a simple dinner or see a movie with on a weeknight.

Josh was on his way to look up her number when the phone rang. "I can't believe this," he said when he heard Lynne's voice. "I was just going to call you."

"Really? My friend Jenny Howard and I were on our way to have coffee at that new café on Seventy-eighth. Would you like to join us?" she asked.

"Sure. The one between First and Second? I've never been there."

"Neither have we. Thought we'd give it a try. Half an hour okay?"

"Just right. See you there."

"Great. And Josh?"

"Yes?"

"What did you want to talk to me about? I hope you're not canceling our game for tomorrow?"

"No, no. I'm looking forward to beating you."

"Ha! We'll see about that. See you in a bit."

Trust Lynne to come through, Josh thought as he put down the phone. *Maybe I should have agreed to meet this friend of hers a long time ago.* He put his supper dishes in the sink, trying to remember what Lynne had told him about her friend. All he could recall was that she was blond and smart and taught somewhere. That sounded good enough for a start. In his bedroom he splashed on some after-shave and grabbed his favorite old leather jacket from the closet.

"Is that him?" Jenny whispered to Lynne.

"Uh-huh."

"You've been holding out, Farrell. Is he as good as he looks?"

Lynne had never seen Josh in anything but squash clothes or a business suit. In jeans and that leather jacket—worn to a sheen and so soft and supple it fitted him like a glove—he looked rugged, strong and sexy. She couldn't remember having thought of Josh as sexy before. Attractive certainly, but not someone to set your pulse racing, as she was surprised to find hers was now. "Better," Lynne answered. She raised her hand to wave to Josh and he smiled back at her and made his way to their table.

"Hi," he said to Jenny, holding out his hand. "I'm Josh Simmons." *And you are gorgeous,* he thought to himself.

Just Friends

Jenny shook his hand and introduced herself, and Josh sat down opposite the two women. "Hi there, Lynnie," he said, reaching across the table to cuff her gently on the chin.

"Hello," Lynne said. Her pulse had settled down to normal, but she felt inexplicably miffed at Josh, as if she'd been passed over at a dance for her prettier girlfriend. She told herself to stop being silly, that Josh was just being his usual friendly outgoing self.

There was a brief awkward silence while the three grinned vacantly at one another, no one sure exactly what was going to come next. Then they all started to talk at once.

"Shall we—"
"Lynne said—"
"Do you—"

They all laughed self-consciously and fell silent again.

"What were you going to say, Jenny?" Josh asked, taking the opportunity to look more closely at her. Even in the dim light of the café he could see the creaminess of her complexion and how her sweater—a soft blue heathery thing with some purple flecks—brought out the blue of her eyes.

"It's not important. You go ahead," Jenny said.

"No, please. You first."

"Who's on first?" Lynne interjected. "I'm beginning to think I'm in an Abbott and Costello movie."

Josh and Jenny both laughed, more freely this time. "I was only going to ask Josh if he liked opera," she said. "It's a pretty obvious question around here." The walls of the café were lined with pictures of opera singers and an opera recording was playing softly in the background.

"I'm not a particular fan," Josh answered. "But I do like classical music, especially chamber music."

"Really?" Lynne said. "I never knew that. I'm quite fond of chamber music myself."

"I guess it never came up," Josh said. He looked across the table at Lynne. She didn't look so bad herself tonight, in a tight white turtleneck and faded denim jacket. Usually after squash her hair hung neatly around her chin, but now she had swept it back and fastened it behind her ears with two ivory combs. Some pretty wisps framed her face. She looked more relaxed and comfortable than she did dressed to go to the office or beat him at squash.

The waitress approached and they ordered cappuccinos and a plate of cookies to nibble.

"When I was in Italy—"

"When were you in Italy?" Josh interrupted Lynne.

"Between my junior and senior years in college. I took a summer course in art history in Florence."

"You never told me that."

"I guess it never came up," Lynne echoed.

"I thought you two knew each other pretty well," Jenny remarked.

"We do," Lynne and Josh said simultaneously and emphatically.

"We just don't have all the facts straight," Josh added with a crooked smile.

"There must be a lot of things we don't know about each other. Not just you and me, Josh, but Jenny and me, too. Of course you and Jenny don't know anything about each other. Except what I've told you, which isn't very much." Lynne looked back and forth from one friend to the other. She was sitting with two people she'd assumed she knew rather well, but how well could you ever know someone you saw only infrequently, who occupied only a small corner of your life?

"Why don't we each tell something we think no one would ever have guessed about us?" Jenny suggested with a mischievous twinkle in her eye. "I'm sure it will be very revealing."

"But you and Josh hardly know each other," Lynne said.

"No, but I've formed an impression. And I'm sure you've formed one of me, Josh."

I sure have, Josh said to himself. *And I'd like to know you better.* With her delicate looks he'd expected Jenny to be shy, even a shade coy perhaps. She was anything but. And he wouldn't mind hearing something new about Lynne, either. It bothered him, not having known that they shared an interest in chamber music. They might have taken in a few concerts together, shared some records or tapes. How many more opportunities had he missed to deepen their friendship?

"It sounds like fun," Lynne said. "But we should have some ground rules. No deep dark secrets."

"No," Jenny agreed. "But something unusual, surprising, even intriguing." Her eyes held a look of challenge.

"All right," Josh said, looking first at Lynne, then Jenny. "Who's on first?"

"Jenny," Lynne said quickly. "It was her idea."

Jenny took a cookie from the plate the waitress had just deposited and munched it with tantalizing slowness. Then she took a sip of her coffee and a few more bites of cookie.

"Any century, Jen," Lynne baited. "Having trouble thinking of something?"

"No."

"Then out with it," Josh said.

"I speak fluent Finnish," Jenny declared. Then she rattled off a few sentences in a gutteral Nordic-sounding language.

Lynne started to laugh and turned to Josh. "How do we know this is Finnish? How do we know this isn't gibberish? Do you know what Finnish sounds like?"

"The closest I've been to Finland," Josh said, "is England. And they sound pretty much like us. Why don't we trust her on it? Or better yet, why don't we test her? Say 'I like reindeer stew,' in Finnish."

Jenny giggled and reeled off a long sentence. "My mother's a Finn, and she wanted us kids to know the language, so she always spoke to us in Finnish. Of course my poor father hardly understands a word." Jenny went on to tell about her visits with her mother's relatives in Finland.

They never got to finish the game. Josh and Lynne asked Jenny lots of questions, and they laughed and joked about the answers. Then the conversation looped around to their own travels, their hilarious mishaps and exciting moments. Jenny had just said something about it being Josh's or Lynne's turn to play when the waitress came over to tell them that the café was closing in fifteen minutes, at midnight.

"It's not that late," Lynne declared. "It couldn't be."

"But it is," Jenny said. "And I've got to be in the office early tomorrow for a departmental meeting."

"And we've got a squash game in the morning," Josh reminded Lynne.

The three walked to Second Avenue together, and Josh hailed a taxi for Jenny. As one pulled up, Jenny threw her arms around Lynne. "Good night. Thanks for dinner. I'd like to return the favor soon."

"Anytime," Lynne said, giving her a squeeze.

Josh helped Jenny into the cab. "I hope to see you again."

"That would be nice," she answered with a particularly warm smile and pulled the door shut.

The cab sped off and Josh said, "I'll walk you home." They started up Second Avenue, saying nothing, but walking in step with each other naturally. After a few moments, Josh took Lynne's arm and linked it through his own, patting her hand briefly.

It was warm for late September, the air damp, almost balmy, the sort of night that made you feel summer would go on forever, that fall and winter would never arrive. It was not just the night that was warm and promising for Lynne. Her feelings for Josh had never been as warm or as cozy as they were now. Nor had her feelings for Jenny. Tonight had been special, a master class in the joys, the importance of friendships and their power to enrich your life.

"If we'd gotten our chance to play the game," Josh said, interrupting her reverie, "what were you going to reveal?"

"I hadn't thought of anything, but believe me, I couldn't have come up with anything like Jenny's Finnish." She added a string of mock-Finnish gibberish.

Josh answered her in kind and they both giggled like children. "Sometime you and I should get together and Finnish—" he emphasized the word heavily so Lynne would be sure to get his pun "—the game."

Lynne groaned and rolled her eyes at him.

"But seriously, why don't you come over to my place one evening? We can listen to some chamber music, and I cook a 'company meal' that's even edible."

"I'd like that," Lynne replied.

He put his arms around her for a hug. "Good night, Lynnie," he said.

Lynne leaned against him, her head on his chest, and gave him a hard squeeze. "Good night, Josh," she said softly. His arms felt good: strong, accepting, undemanding. She liked the feeling, so different from the pressures she often felt with men she was dating.

"I'll see you in court, Farrell." He bent down and bussed her on both cheeks. "And you'd better be sharp," he challenged.

"So had you," she shot back as he started down the street.

Lynne took her keys from her jacket pocket and was about to unlock the street door when she heard Josh calling her. She turned around.

"Is Jenny's number in the book?" he asked.

"Under J. Howard, on Mercer," she answered matter-of-factly and turned her key in the lock. But on her way up the stairs an unexpected pang of something suspiciously like jealousy assailed her sharply and suddenly. She stopped on the landing. What was going on here? Hadn't she brought Josh and Jenny together so that they'd start seeing each other? *Cut it out,* she told herself firmly. *Feelings like this have been known to ruin a friendship. A friendship? I've got two—two important ones—at stake here.*

Lynne let herself into her apartment and quickly prepared for bed. But that suspicious little pang kept poking at her. She tossed and turned and when sleep finally came, it was restless and fraught with dreams she could not remember in the morning.

3

"I'M GLAD WE'RE NOT on different sides of the table every week. I'm getting too old for this sort of thing," Alan Parker said to Lynne as the weekly editorial meeting broke up. He was the son of one of the company's founders, and handled the editorial side of the business while Sam Hamilton, son of the other founder, took care of company administration. Every Wednesday morning at ten he assembled his staff to discuss new acquisitions and the progress of books already on Parker and Hamilton's list. This morning there had been a lengthy debate about whether or not to bid for the latest novel by a well-known author who was in the market for a new publisher.

The property was frankly more commercial than most of the fiction on P & H's list, but Alan Parker saw enough genuine merit in the book and its author to favor bidding seriously for it. The company, he said, could only stay competitive with the big-money publishers by beating them at their own game once in a while.

When a man who in his forty-five year career had edited some of the most famous, controversial and important books of his era expressed an opinion strongly, few in the room challenged it, even when the man himself invited opposing points of view.

But Lynne, although she'd had no intention of doing so at the start of the meeting, had become his most vocal opponent in the course of the discussion. She argued that the company should continue to put its best efforts and financial resources into the books they traditionally had done so well with—the ones everyone else in town had rejected through lack of foresight or courage, and which then went on to head the best-seller lists for a year when published by Parker and Hamilton. Backed by her in-depth knowledge of the company—she'd been there longer than anyone on the editorial staff except for Alan Parker and one of the other senior editors—she'd made some excellent points. But not enough of them to change Alan's mind.

"You have become an admirable opponent," Alan complimented.

Lynne barely managed to suppress a self-satisfied smile. Alan Parker was as parsimonious with compliments as Sam Hamilton was with raises. "You've only yourself to blame," she reminded him as she gathered up the files, notebook and pen she had brought to the meeting. "You trained me. And you haven't turned into an old softie overnight. You're still pretty tough yourself."

"For an old geezer," he said with a smile and an avuncular pat on her shoulder. "If you ever want to get out of publishing, you might try devil's advocacy."

"As long as I don't have to wear a red suit," Lynne returned with a grin. "I look terrible in that color." Although she and Alan might find themselves at loggerheads from time to time, their working relationship was one of the things that had kept her at the company. She'd started work as Alan's editorial assistant, and he'd been her mentor as she climbed the editorial ladder. She would be very sorry to see him retire, as he was scheduled to do in only a few weeks. Not only would she miss him, but she would be losing her chief ally in the company.

Lynne was halfway to her office when she remembered that she hadn't had a chance to bring up the book on cross-country skiing that she wanted to buy. It was disappointing, because she'd stayed late at the office the day before to have the profit projections ready for the meeting. But more to the point, she was having lunch with the agent today and had promised her an answer. Now it would have to wait until next week, by which time the agent would have submitted the book to someone else—unless Lynne could convince her not to. She wondered if she had any favors she could call in from Lydia Hastings.

"That was a long one," her assistant, Tom Doran, said as she reached his desk, which was positioned in an alcove in the hallway across from her door. In his outstretched hand was a sheaf of pink message slips. Beneath the hedge of curly red hair that covered his forehead, his blue eyes were avid for news of what had gone on in the meeting. Tom, fresh out of college, had only been with Parker and Hamilton since June, but Lynne knew it wouldn't be long before he was sitting in on editorial meetings, either here or at another house.

"It looks like Alan is going to enter the fray," Lynne reported with a philosophical note in her voice. She'd had her say, now it was her job to support the house in its decisions.

"That ought to raise the decibel level around here a few points," Tom said eagerly. "And what about the ski book?" he asked with affected nonchalance.

"Sorry, kid, I didn't even have time to bring it up."

Tom's face drooped with disappointment. "That means we're probably going to lose it." His personal stake in this project was high. He'd read the proposal first and recommended it to Lynne. Since he knew a lot about the subject she had offered to let him edit the book—with her supervision, of course—if the acquisition was approved.

"Probably. But I'll work on Lydia Hastings at lunch. We may still have a shot. By the way, where are we eating?" She had left it up to Tom to settle the lunch plans while she was in the meeting.

"I've booked your usual table at Lutèce," he said blithely. Tom's sense of humor never deserted him for long.

"Right," Lynne said with a chortle. "And send the accounting department into orbit." Lutèce was one of the city's most famous and exclusive French restaurants, and had the prices to prove it.

"I got you a table at the City Café on Second. Ms Hastings said she'd prefer something light and they have good rabbit food." Tom wrinkled his nose and made a few rapid chewing movements with his mouth.

"Just wait a few years, my friend. You won't always be able to inhale a whole pizza for lunch." Lynne waved the message slips at him. "Anything in here I should take care of before I retire to my hutch?"

"Mona Lewis in publicity. There's another snag on the author tour for Jack Benedetti."

"Unbelievable. Why me?" she asked, rolling her eyes heavenward. She'd had a hard enough time getting Benedetti—a police officer who'd devised an excercise program that had been adopted by all the uniformed services in the city—to go on tour anyway. And now she was calling him every day with changes.

Inside her office, Lynne had the phone in hand and Mona Lewis on the other end before she'd even sat down in her chair. In the half hour since her call to Lynne, Mona had managed to solve the Benedetti problem, but had another query about a press release she was writing for one of Lynne's other projects. Lynne had hardly put down the phone when Tom called in through the open door of her office.

"Jenny Howard on three."

"Got it." Lynne picked up the phone and leaned back in her chair. "Hi. What's up?" It was unusual for Jenny to call her at the office. Her days were as busy as Lynne's and neither of them had much time to spend on personal matters during a workday.

"I had a few minutes between classes and I thought I might catch you before you went out to lunch. How are you?"

"Overworked and underpaid."

"And loving every minute of it."

"Guilty as charged," Lynne said with a laugh.

"I won't keep you long. I only called to say that your friend Josh phoned me last night. We're having dinner on Saturday." There was a slight hesitation in Jenny's speech. "I thought I should tell you. I'm not quite sure why."

Once again, as it had when Josh had asked her for Jenny's number, that same suspicious little pang of—she hated to call it jealousy, but couldn't think of a better word at the moment—pricked her. But this time it was tinged with something else, a kind of possessiveness, a feeling that Josh should have told her he was going to ask Jenny out. Of course she could voice none of these concerns to Jenny, and so tried to sound as pleased for her friends as she thought she should be. "Because I introduced you? Don't be silly, Jen. This was the whole point, wasn't it?"

"Lynne, are you sure there's nothing going on between you and Josh?"

"If there is," Lynne said heartily, "it's the best-kept secret in town. Even we don't know about it. Look, Jen, I've got to run. Late for a lunch date. Have a good time on Saturday. I'll talk to you next week."

Lynne hung up the phone slowly and got up from her desk. After her full morning she'd felt charged with the energy that came from being in the thick of the action, but suddenly she felt as if she'd stopped in midstep and was caught in a freeze frame like someone in a film. The projector had stopped whirring; her brain, her body was at a standstill.

She stood for a time in front of the window, watching the cold fall rain pelt the glass. Fifteen stories below, the gnarl of traffic was inching its way in fits and starts up Third Avenue. Lynne had never understood why the rain slowed things down so much, why the traffic couldn't adjust to a little water. That's all it was, a little water.

And what had stopped her cold was only a little.... A little what, she asked herself. But the answer was as tied up inside her as the traffic was below. She turned resolutely and slipped her raincoat from its hanger on the back of her door. On her way to the elevator she forced herself to think only of the problem at hand: how she was going to convince Lydia Hastings to let her hold on to that skiing book for another week.

LYNNE WAS AWAY from her desk late the following afternoon when Josh called to cancel their Friday-morning game. Unable to find a partner on such short notice, she went to the courts alone the next morning and spent the time perfecting her serve and her winning shots. Usually she enjoyed a solitary workout, but this time it felt strange being on the court without Josh. She missed their banter and the mental and physical exertion of their games, especially now that they were so evenly matched. After showering and changing she went straight to the office, where she worked until long after everyone else had left for the weekend.

As she packed her briefcase and prepared to go home she had the feeling she was trying to delay the start of the weekend, although there was no reason for her to do that. In fact, she should have been looking forward to it: she had a date on Saturday night with a literary agent she'd met at a publication party the week before, and on Sunday she was going on a bicycle tour sponsored by a local cycling club. The weather service was predicting a splendid fall weekend, but Lynne felt like she was facing two days of late-February gloom. Shaking away the feeling as vigorously as a dog shakes off water after a romp in a pond, Lynne flicked off the lights in her office and made her way to the elevator.

"YOU SEEM AWFULLY QUIET TODAY," Josh said to Lynne on Tuesday morning as they walked from the squash club to the Apollo. "Not even crowing over that last shot you made. What a tie breaker that was. I thought I had you...and then whack! That would have been a home run if we'd been playing baseball." When Lynne didn't answer for a few seconds Josh added, "Are you okay, Lynne?"

"Just a little tired, I guess. I stayed up late last night reading."

"Manuscripts?"

"For a change, no. I actually read a published book, with printed words, the pages all bound together between covers. The real thing." After pushing aside a tedious manuscript, she'd dozed off on the sofa around eleven, but once in bed she hadn't been able to sleep. She had lain there staring into the darkness, wondering what she was going to say to Josh this morning. Should she bring up his date with Jenny? Pretend she hadn't known anything about it? How should she react if and when he told her about it? Should she tell him how she had felt when Jenny had phoned? The questions ran around and around in her mind like mice in a maze with no exit. Finally, the possibility of either answers or sleep banished, Lynne had switched on the light to read.

"I hope it was something good," Josh prodded, looking sideways at Lynne as he held open the door of the coffee shop for her. She didn't seem like herself this morning. He couldn't remember having to drag conversation out of her before.

"Not really," she answered with a shrug. "A murder mystery. I figured it out halfway through—"

"But you had to stay up to make sure you were right," Josh interrupted with a knowing grin. The grin widened when he saw that he had elicited a small smile from her.

Rose greeted them warmly as they neared the cash register. "Good morning. No picnic today?"

"It's getting a bit chilly out there, Rose," Josh said, stopping beside her chair. Lynne had walked on a couple of paces before she'd realized he'd stopped. She didn't feel like making small talk with Rose this morning and she particularly wanted to avoid any comparisons with characters in a romantic novel. So she remained where she was while Josh chatted with the cheerful woman.

"Don't worry, you two," she said with a broad smile as Josh stepped away. "Spring will be here before you know it. There's a booth set up in the back. Enjoy your breakfast."

"Thanks," Josh replied. "You're very talkative this morning," he whispered to Lynne as they walked to the empty booth.

"Nothing to say," Lynne whispered back with a shrug.

When the waiter came to take their orders, Josh made a few jokes with him, but as soon as he left silence drifted in on them again like threatening clouds at a summer outing.

"So," Josh said a shade too brightly, "what did you do this weekend?"

"Oh, nothing much," Lynne answered automatically, her first impulse being to steer the talk away from weekend activities. But in fact Sunday had been one of the most interesting and unusual days she'd ever spent in New York and she couldn't help mentioning it. "On Sunday I went on a bike tour with a cycling club." At his coaxing she began to describe the day to Josh.

The cyclists had pedaled down to the tip of Manhattan and put their bikes on the Staten Island ferry, then they toured New York's least-known borough, ending up at a small museum that housed a fine collection of Tibetan art.

Lynne had not talked to anyone about the trip, and as she spoke her natural enthusiasm took over. "It was fantastic, Josh. One minute I was on my bike, the next I was in Tibet." Their breakfasts were served and Lynne didn't miss a syllable of her story as she buttered a triangle of toast and took a small bite. "The museum looks just like a temple both inside and out, and behind it there are terraced gardens with statues of Buddha and stone elephants poking out from between the shrubs. We brought sack lunches and ate them outside at a long stone table. It was so tranquil I almost forgot I was anywhere near the city. I'd love to show it to you sometime."

The invitation had been spontaneous, but after she'd spoken she realized how much she'd thought of Josh on Sunday, wishing he was there to share her delightful adventure.

Josh smiled happily at her over the rim of his coffee cup. "That would be fun," he said. Lynne described things so well he always wanted to see them himself. Her face was so fluid and expressive when she was talking about something that had caught her quickly aroused interest. Telling the story also seemed to have brought her out of the blue funk she'd been in earlier. "It's nice to have my old Lynnie back," he said tenderly. "I couldn't figure out where you were before."

At his words Lynne's stomach began performing like an Olympic gymnast, tumbling and vaulting and flipping. Something in the way he'd said "my Lynnie" had set it off. But suddenly reality hit. *My pal*, my *buddy* was what he had meant. "I don't understand what you're saying," she remarked testily. "I haven't been anywhere."

"Except to Tibet. Where few Westerners have ever been," Josh said, imitating the voice of the narrator of an old-fashioned adventure film. "And where only the high Dilly Dally Lama knows the secret of the Blue Over You Buddha. It was this secret that Michigan Smith was determined to uncover...."

Lynne relented first with a smile and then with a delayed chuckle. Trust Josh to make her laugh even when she didn't want to. She relaxed a little and ate some of her breakfast. *Stop being crazy*, she told herself firmly. *There's no reason to get all tense and nervous just because one of my friends had a date with another of my friends.*

"So who'd you go to Tibet with?" Josh asked, forking up some scrambled eggs.

"I told you, a bike club. Someone put a notice up on the bulletin board at work and it sounded like fun. Why?"

"I thought you might have gone with a friend... or a date. Say, didn't you tell me you were seeing that literary agent on Saturday?"

Just when the conversation seemed to be getting onto an easier footing, Josh had to bring up the subject of weekend dates. Lynne felt herself tense up again. "I guess I did," she answered listlessly as she thought back to Saturday night.

Just Friends

She had expected the evening to go so well. As she'd gone about her Saturday rounds—supermarket, dry cleaner, hardware store—she had thought of all the reasons that it should. She and her date were in the same business; they knew a lot of the same people. When they'd first met she'd found him very attractive. He'd reminded her a little of Josh with his engaging smile and quick wit. But both had flagged on closer inspection; they did not become deeper or more dazzling as those traits did in Josh.

But the real trouble lay less with the man than with her own expectations. She had so many of them these days. Whenever she met a new man she found her expectations growing almost without her conscious help, the way a plant grows from a windborne seed that is dropped on the ground and watered by the rain. No one does anything, it just sprouts. From one small expectation she found entire dreams blossoming. Dreams that disintegrated into a thousand fragments when they collided with reality. As they had Saturday night.

"Earth to Lynne, earth to Lynne," Josh was intoning. When she redirected her attention to him he said, "I've heard people sound more enthusiastic about going to the dentist. It couldn't have been that bad."

"It wasn't that it was bad," Lynne replied. "It just wasn't what I had expected. We went to a Tex-Mex restaurant down in Soho. The food was good, and he was nice enough. But all he wanted to talk about was how many fantastic contracts he'd negotiated for his authors. I deal with the business of books all week, Josh. On Saturday night I want to talk about what's in them, not how they get into the bookstores."

"I'm sorry you didn't have a better time."

"Yeah, me too."

Now Josh let silence fall between them. There was a long pause and then he blurted out, "Look, Lynne, I've been trying to avoid this all morning, but speaking of dates, I saw your friend Jenny on Saturday night." Josh put down his fork. It collided with the knife and both utensils fell to the floor with a clatter. Josh mumbled something under his breath, picked up the silverware and laid it carefully across his empty plate. He looked up sheepishly. "I don't know why, but telling you about this makes me nervous."

"Turnabout is fair play," Lynne pointed out. "I've told you all about my disaster. You shouldn't feel nervous telling me about yours."

"It wasn't a disaster at all," Josh rejoined rapidly.

"You needn't get defensive," Lynne said, jumping to her own defense. "I didn't mean that the way it came out. I want to know all about it," Lynne plunged on. "What did you do? Where did you go? What did you talk about?"

"We had dinner at an Italian restaurant on Sullivan Street—pasta, Veal Scallopini, red wine, espresso. *Squisito!*" Josh pursed his lips and kissed his fingertips in the gesture of a proud Italian chef. He mugged for approval like an applause-starved vaudevillian and Lynne was hard pressed not to give him a smile.

"Between bites we mostly talked about Jenny's doctoral thesis. I can give you a blow-by-blow account, but it's pretty boring stuff for anyone without a deep and abiding affection for financial statistics—like me and Jenny."

Lynne turned away as he uttered those last four words. The way he strung them together made it sound as if he and Jenny were an old established couple.

Josh could not help but notice her discomfort. "Are you sure we should be talking about this, Lynne?"

"We've always talked about our dates before," she maintained staunchly. "Why should this be any different?"

"Because it is, and you know it. You're going to go and have dinner with Jenny and she'll be able to compare notes on what I said to you—"

"Josh!" Lynne was indignant. "How could you even think that I'd repeat anything you said to me in confidence?"

"It's not that you'd do it on purpose, but.... Well, when friends talk freely things tend to seep out."

"I'm really hurt, Josh. I thought you trusted me."

"Trust you?" Josh reached across the table and covered her hand with his. "I trust you more than any friend I've ever had."

Lynne looked up at him in surprise. She searched his face closely, touched, pleased and even a little shaken by his revelation. "For true?" she asked softly.

"For true."

"More coffee, folks?" The waiter stood beside the booth brandishing a steaming glass carafe. When Josh pulled his hand away from Lynne's the waiter gave him a well-worn smile that said he'd seen a lot more than hand holding in his time. He replenished their cups and moved on to the next table.

Without asking, Josh tipped the cream pitcher over Lynne's cup, knowing just how much to pour. She looked at him affectionately, thinking that there were too few people in the world who knew how she took her coffee.

"As I was saying," Josh began, stirring cream and sugar into his own coffee, "before we so rudely interrupted ourselves by having an argu—"

"A difference of opinion," Lynne supplied evenly.

Josh gave her a courtly nod. "A difference of opinion. Shall I go on?"

"Of course," Lynne replied, confident that nothing he could say would ruffle her.

"Well, then. After our feast, Jenny and I decided we needed some exercise, so we strolled around the Village for a while. We happened to find ourselves near the Blue Note just as the first set was starting, so we went in. You should have seen Jenny, getting into that music," Josh said, savoring the memory with apparent relish. "She's so surprising. With that face and that hair you'd expect her to behave like some kind of angel. But she's got a good healthy dose of the devil in her. She's a lot of fun to be with."

"Mmm," Lynne replied noncommittally. Despite her expectations—there was that word again—she found herself trying to keep from feeling miffed by Josh's praise of Jenny, even though his words echoed her own frequent thoughts about her friend.

"And then, since it was getting late, we went back to Jenny's pl—"

The last of Lynne's cool melted like an ice cube in the July sun. "You can finish right there, Josh. I don't think I want to hear any more." Lynne began to fumble for her briefcase and purse and slid over to the end of the booth.

Josh reached out a hand to stop her. "I only meant that I saw her back to her apartment. I apologize for the fact that my parents raised me to have some manners," he said hotly.

"They did?" Lynne glared at his hand on her arm. "You were right before," she said, shaking off Josh's hand and taking her raincoat down from the hook beside the booth. "We shouldn't be talking about this."

"Not if it gets you so bent out of shape," he retorted. "I'm sorry," he added almost immediately. "Don't rush off this way. I've got a rough enough day ahead without having to hash this over in my mind, wondering what went wrong."

Lynne crumpled onto the edge of the seat. "Me, too. I'm sorry, Josh. I guess it's because I care about both of you."

"Why don't we agree that we won't talk about this anymore?" Josh suggested.

"Fine with me."

She was not expecting it, but Josh reached over and took her hand again. "Friends?" he asked. His gaze burrowed deep inside her. He seemed to be asking for a vow, not merely an answer.

"Friends," Lynne answered solemnly. He squeezed her hand hard and she squeezed back, stifling the urge to stand and stretch out her arms to him. Finally she slipped her hand out of his. "I'd better be getting to the office," she said gently. "Are you coming?"

"You go on. I think I'll finish my coffee. And breakfast is on me this morning, Lynne."

"Thanks." She accepted the conciliatory gesture with a nod.

"None needed. After the stunning victory I fully intend to have on Friday morning, you'll be buying me breakfast," he challenged not quite playfully.

"I wouldn't take bets on that if I were you," Lynne said lightly as she hoisted her gear. "See you Friday, Josh."

"Same time, same place."

His words echoed in her head as she left the coffee shop. *But it's not the same,* she said to herself. And it hadn't been for a while, not since Josh came back from his vacation last month. But there was no going back now. As much as she regretted the changes in their comfy cozy relationship, she had to admit that she was equally anxious to see what lay beyond the next bend of the bumpy—but new—road that stretched before her.

4

"Great seats," Lynne said to Jenny as the usherette showed them to two aisle places smack in the middle of the orchestra. The Broadway show they were going to see was a "hot ticket"—sold out for a month in advance—and featured a popular Hollywood actor said to be giving the performance of a lifetime. Not only were tickets difficult to come by, they were very expensive. Because of the high ticket prices and the necessity to plan so far in advance, Lynne would probably have missed the production altogether, but Jenny had been given the tickets gratis by a colleague who was unable to use them.

When Jenny had called late in the afternoon, Lynne almost pleaded a previous date, even though she'd had none, because she was so nervous about seeing her friend. It was only yesterday morning that she and Josh had sat in the Apollo talking about their date. Lynne was still off-balance from that encounter, and she would have preferred not to see Jenny so soon. But putting it off would only give her time to develop preconceived notions about what would happen and how both she and Jenny would feel. So she'd accepted the invitation. But when she'd met Jenny in the theater lobby just a few minutes before, she had felt an uneasiness between them, a sense of restraint, even a note of caution.

Trying to banish the bothersome undercurrent, Lynne asked, "Who does your friend know?" She flashed Jenny an "okay" signal and Jenny smiled, a little too broadly, but a genuine smile nonetheless.

"Beats me," Jenny replied, handing Lynne one of the programs the usherette had just given her. "I didn't ask too many questions. Just took the tickets and ran."

This time Jenny's grin was less strained and Lynne breathed an inward sigh of relief. Maybe the evening wouldn't be as difficult as she had thought. As she settled herself in the plush red velvet seat Lynne couldn't remember when she last had seats this good at the theater. Usually she sat in the balcony or relied on the half-price ticket booth in Times Square for seats that tended to be far to the sides or the rear of the theater.

With the growing sense of anticipation she always felt before the start of a performance, she listened to the buzz of voices, the snaps of purse clasps, the jingle of jewelry, the rustle of pages being turned in programs, and the different laughs—chortles, chuckles, giggles, guffaws—that rose above the other sounds like a descant in a piece of choral music. There was the smell of hundreds of different perfumes in the warm air, mixed with a hint of ink and crisp paper from the slickly printed playbills. The houselights began to dim and the crowd quieted down. There was a moment of crackling silence and darkness before the play began. Lynne relaxed even more and waited to be swept away by the magic of the theater.

"ISN'T IT WONDERFUL?" Jenny breathed as the lights went up for the intermission. She told Lynne how much she liked the acting and how intriguing she found the play.

"Well...." Lynne hedged. Her reaction had been quite unlike Jenny's. She thought the play not very worthy except as a star vehicle, and that the star had surrounded himself with obviously mediocre performers in order to make himself stand out all the more. She'd found her attention wandering throughout, and more often than not it landed on Josh and his evening with Jenny. "I can't say I was transported."

Jenny's eyebrows shot up. "Really?"

Lynne shrugged apologetically. Had she paid for her ticket herself, or felt less guilty about the thoughts she'd been having while sitting in the darkness, she would have felt no compunction to apologize for her feelings, but as Jenny's guest she felt somehow obligated to like the play. Until she remembered that Jenny hadn't paid for her ticket, either. Nor had she so much as mentioned Josh. It was her own imagination that was running the show here tonight. Lynne rose decisively. "Let's get something to drink. I'm parched."

Jenny agreed and they made their way slowly up the aisle and then up the stairs to the mezzanine-level bar. The crowd was four-deep around the bar, but Lynne and Jenny sidled over to the edge and managed to get two ginger ales from the overworked barman.

"It always amazes me," Lynne said, as they threaded their way to an unoccupied two-foot-square spot of carpet near the wall, "that they never have more than one bartender to deal with all these hundreds of people."

"Uneconomical," Jenny remarked. "Theater producers are in a bind. Costs keep rising and there's no way to expand their income. They can't put more seats in the theater or schedule more performances per week, so ticket prices go up and services are cut back." Jenny took a sip of her drink. "And they water down the soda," she said with a grimace. "But that's life in the big city, the price we pay for being 'where it's at.' Would you ever move away?"

"Only as far as the suburbs," Lynne answered. "It's hard to be in publishing and not live in New York. Besides, I love it. I wouldn't mind having a weekend retreat somewhere, but I don't think I'd be happy living very far from the city. Are you thinking of going somewhere else—when you finish your dissertation, that is?"

"I wouldn't mind," Jenny said, "being someplace where there was more open space and a less-hectic pace. Unfortunately, most of the business schools where I'd like to teach are decidedly urban. It's funny, Josh and I were talking about this on Saturday night. He feels pretty much the way you do, but you must know that. I really have to thank you for introducing me to him, Lynne. I had a wonderful time on Saturday. Josh is a super guy, just the kind some lucky woman should marry and live happily ever after with. We had so much to talk about. I think he's going to be able to help me with some information that I need for my thesis, and I'm certainly looking forward to—"

The lights began to blink, signaling the start of the second act. "We'd better get back downstairs," Lynne interrupted, glad for an excuse not to have to respond to Jenny's gushing comments. The subject of Josh had hovered over them like one of those meddlesome gods in Greek literature, just waiting to see what dissension he could sow in the human ranks. She could just imagine the little imp, rubbing his hands together with glee now. All she wanted to do was get out of his range. She turned toward the stairs.

"We're going to have to talk about this sometime," Jenny said, putting a restraining hand on Lynne's forearm.

"Now is hardly the time," Lynne answered. "And I don't know if we should talk about it. Josh and I got on the subject yesterday and had the first argument we've ever had. If I start talking about it to you, I'm going to feel like the monkey in the middle." Lynne looked around and saw that they were nearly the last people to start back to their seats. "We'd better be going," Lynne said again. "And I really do think it would be better if we didn't talk about what goes on between you and Josh. It's none of my business, anyway."

"If that's the way you feel, Lynne," Jenny replied stiffly.

"YOU STILL HAVEN'T RSVP'd about Mr. Parker's retirement ball," Tom reminded her the following morning as they were going over the day's work.

"I know," Lynne said to her assistant. "Don't tell anyone," she confided, "but I don't have a date."

"You're kidding. It's in two weeks, Lynne, and the invitation asks for an answer by Friday. What are you waiting for?"

"Mr. Right," Lynne quipped.

"Forget Mr. Right," Tom advised. "What you

need now is Mr. Okay, Mr. I Can Stand to Spend an Evening With. What about that guy you play squash with? He's not married or anything, is he?"

"Oh, I couldn't...." Lynne protested feebly, wondering why the idea hadn't occurred to her before.

"Well, it's a thought. Now, about the sports nutrition book, can you check with production...."

For once, Lynne left the office at five-thirty, the normal quitting time, planning to cook herself a good supper, relax at home for the evening and get to bed at a reasonable hour. Tomorrow was a squash day, which meant getting up early; she'd also have a chance to ask Josh if he could escort her to Alan's dinner-dance. She had to go, and she couldn't go without an escort. She'd considered the alternatives all day and decided there weren't any. Besides, there were worse prospects than an evening dining and dancing with Josh.

On her way from the bus stop, Lynne stopped at the supermarket, crowded with after-work shoppers, to pick up something for supper. The store was one of the new "gourmet" markets that had begun to spring up around Manhattan. It had, among other features, a special butcher shop in addition to the usual packaged meats; a French bakery with freshly baked breads, croissants and pastries; and a salad bar where you could build the salad of your dreams from a score or more of ingredients.

There was a long line at the butcher counter, so Lynne perused the meat section and decided that boneless chicken breasts would be both quick and a treat. She had a special recipe for cooking them with a lemon-and-parsley sauce. All the packages held enough meat for two people; she would have to freeze the portion she didn't use. After picking up a loaf of French bread she went to the fresh-vegetable section, chose a lemon and a bunch of parsley and then considered possible accompaniments for the chicken: broccoli, string beans, yellow squash, zucchini, a salad? Lynne was just about to reach for a bunch of broccoli when she heard a harsh voice whispering in her ear.

"I know where you can get a great deal on carrots, lady. I got a cousin in the business."

The raspy voice with its heavy Bronx accent made Lynne gasp and instinctively jump away. But then she heard a familiar laugh and looked around to see Josh. He was clutching his blue plastic market basket to his chest, trying to keep from bursting out laughing again.

"You scared the heck out of me," Lynne admonished.

"I know," Josh said guiltily. "Sorry, I couldn't resist."

They both opened their mouths as if to say something and shut them at the same moment. Lynne shook her head. "I was actually going to ask you what you were doing here."

"Me, too," Josh said with a silly grin. He dangled his basket in front of him and pointed to hers. "Looks like we were both caught in the act." He leaned over and rifled through her groceries. "Mmm. Chicken, lemon, parsley. That looks like it might fix up into something quite tasty." He took a long sniff of her loaf of French bread and exhaled as if intoxicated. "Perfume from heaven," he said in a low breathy voice.

On his face was the sort of expression one might expect from the devotee of a cult when in the presence of its leader.

"You look as if you're about to kowtow to it," Lynne told him with a laugh. "But I've got to admit it beats the white squishy stuff that usually passes for bread."

Suddenly Josh stopped clowning around. "You know," he said speculatively, "I just happen to have the perfect veggies for this meal—broccoli and a salad. Why don't we check out together and go cook this at my place? No sense messing up two kitchens. I've got a nice white Burgundy in the refrigerator, so all we need is dessert. If you get in the checkout line I'll dash over to the bakery counter." Without giving her a chance to say yes or no he sped off in the direction of that section.

As she joined the long queue behind one of the cash registers, Lynne wondered if by having Josh so much on her mind the past couple of days she had somehow conjured him up. It was a great coincidence that they'd met over the broccoli at the supermarket. She rarely left the office this early and she knew Josh didn't, either; only her urge for a special meal had made her stop here. She had enough supplies in the cupboard and refrigerator to have fixed herself an everyday meal. *Well,* she thought, feeling a little balloon of excitement begin to inflate inside her, *so much for a quiet evening at home.*

Josh made it back to the line just as the cashier was packing the purchases of the man in front of Lynne. "Since this was my idea, I'll pay for the groceries," he insisted when Lynne took out her wallet to pay for her share.

Out on the street, Lynne turned up her collar against the late-October chill. Not that she was cold. On the contrary, she felt quite warm, flushed almost, but she could still feel the wind blowing at the back of her neck. They covered the few blocks to Josh's apartment quickly, talking mostly about why they had never run into each other at the supermarket before, since both of them had done most of their shopping there once the store had opened the previous spring.

"Fate," Josh declared as they entered the lobby of his building.

"That we didn't meet there before or that we did tonight?" Lynne asked as they waited for the elevator.

"Both," Josh said decisively and ushered her into the elegant old wood-paneled car. The building was very well maintained and Lynne could smell the lemon-oil polish that had been applied to the rich cherry-wood panels.

As she waited for Josh to open the door to his apartment, Lynne realized she had no clear image of what Josh's home would be like. Would she find a designer decor planned down to the position of the magazines on the coffee table, or a room done up in what she called "early-fraternity style"—a mishmash of pieces picked up catch-as-catch-can and objets d'art supplied by breweries and fast-food chains.

Josh switched on the lights in the foyer and Lynne stepped into the apartment. Though the living room was lit only by the reflected light from where they stood, she saw that it held a comfortable assortment of well-made, well-chosen furniture. The couch and easy chairs were covered with a handsome nubby fabric—the couch in coffee brown, the two chairs in a complimentary shade of taupe—and she spied a lovely antique table and chairs in the dining alcove. The room was tidy but clearly lived in by someone who cared about his surroundings. Just looking at it made her feel warm and homey.

"Can I take your coat?" Josh asked. As he helped her slip it off, his hands lingered on her shoulders for a moment. "It's really good to have you here, Lynnie," he said softly.

"Thanks," she said, feeling a little bump of contentment affix itself at the base of her throat. "Not that you gave me much of a choice. You ran off so fast in the market."

"I didn't want to give you a chance to refuse." He turned her around to face him. "We're okay, aren't we? Slate cleared and all that?"

"Sure."

"Good. That's really good." He nodded and smiled sweetly, then touched the back of his fingers gently to her cheek. They were silent for a moment, looking intently at each other until the look was on the verge of becoming something else. Lynne could feel the short distance between them becoming even shorter, but then Josh pulled back. "Well," he began heartily, "no use standing here in the foyer all night. Make yourself comfortable. I'll put the perishables in the fridge and open that bottle of wine."

Josh switched on the overhead track lighting in the living room and adjusted it to cast a soft glow. Lynne collected herself and crossed to the couch. As she waited for Josh, she glanced at the books and periodicals on the coffee and end tables: issues of the *Wall Street Journal* and *The Economist*, financial reports in glossy covers, a half-read paperback open and lying facedown. She inspected its spine. Josh was midway through Joseph Conrad's *Heart of Darkness*. From the looks of the book it was not a first reading.

"I found a wedge of Brie," Josh said to her from the door of the kitchen. He held two glasses of wine in his hands. "It'll be better if we let the cheese warm up for a few minutes." He walked over to the couch and handed her one of the two glasses.

Lynne took a sip and the cold wine coursed down her throat, creating a warm path from her tongue to her stomach. "It's good," she said, sipping again and feeling the inner glow intensify.

"Mmm," Josh agreed, looking down at her and taking a long draft of wine. "You look very pretty in that sweater," he said quietly. "It makes your eyes look almost blue." He sat down on the sofa very close to her.

Lynne looked down at her sweater, almost as if she'd forgotten what she was wearing. It was her blue-green angora with the cowl neck—one of her favorites. She held fast to her wineglass, conscious that Josh's eyes were riveted on her. Something very new was going on, something very different from anything that had ever passed between her and Josh, but also in some magical way a logical extension of what had come before.

Suddenly Josh bolted off the couch, moving so quickly that it rocked and Lynne felt a jolt. It was almost as if she had been in a taxi that had screeched to a halt at a traffic light. "How about some music?" he asked, his voice reverberating in the room. "I just bought the new release by the Primavera Quartet.

Have you heard it?" He hurried to the stereo that was set up in the wall unit across from the couch.

"No," Lynne said, catching her breath. "But I'd love to. I've read some very good reviews of it," she added, knowing she sounded like someone who was making conversation at a cocktail party. "And I heard them play at Tully last spring," she babbled on.

"I've never heard them live. I wanted to go, but by the time I got around to ordering tickets they were sold out." Josh slipped the record from its jacket, cleaned it carefully and put it on the turntable. He was about to start back over to the couch, but stopped in midstep. "Would you mind if I changed my clothes? I can't stand hanging around in a suit after work if I don't have to."

"We don't have to stand on ceremony, Josh."

Josh suddenly looked worried and peered down warily at his feet, lifting one and then the other gingerly. "Ceremony? Where? I don't see any ceremonies down here. I couldn't possibly have been standing on one, could I?"

"Get out of here, you goof." Lynne sat back on the couch, kicked off her shoes and put her feet up on the coffee table. The wine, or something, was beginning to get to her, and she leaned her head back and shut her eyes, drinking in the soothing strains of Haydn that filled the room.

In his bedroom, Josh stripped off his suit, hung it up and dropped his shirt into the straw laundry hamper on the floor of the closet. He'd come very close to kissing Lynne just then. The urge had come out of nowhere, and it seemed to be prompted by nothing more than seeing her in the dimly lit room, a glass of wine in hand, looking so soft and touchable in that sweater. She'd seemed a natural part of the room and he'd wanted to embrace her, embrace the whole cozy picture.

He didn't understand what had gotten into him. A romantic scene was not what he'd had in mind when he saw her in the market. Or if it had been he wasn't aware of it. On examination he decided that the feelings were not entirely welcome. He didn't want to lose his friendship with Lynne only to be left with yet another ex-girlfriend. He pulled on a pair of jeans and took a sport shirt from a bureau drawer. It occurred to him briefly that it might be possible to have both a friendship and a romance, but he rejected that quickly. Friends were one thing and romance quite another. It was only the circumstances—wine, soft lights, the end of the day—that had made him want to kiss her. And Lynne was also a damned attractive woman. Only a blind fool would have missed that. But that was no reason to go spoiling a perfectly good friendship.

Josh returned to the living room via the kitchen bearing a basket of crackers and the plate of Brie that had been warming on the counter. "Cheese?" he inquired cheerily of Lynne, placing the plate and basket on the coffee table and taking a seat in one of the easy chairs that flanked the couch. "I don't know about you, but I'm starving."

When she heard Josh approach, Lynne opened her eyes and sat up. For a moment she had a strange feeling, as if like Rip van Winkle she'd been asleep for a very long time, and in that time the whole world had changed.

From Josh's outstretched hand, Lynne accepted a

cheese-topped cracker. As she nibbled it she concentrated on shaking off the residue of the spell she had been under for those few minutes, minutes that were retreating quickly into some distant place in time. She let Josh's talk of music pull her fully into the present and soon they were conversing animatedly about the upcoming season in chamber music.

After a while Josh expressed the need for something more substantial to eat than cheese, and they went into the kitchen and fixed supper together. Lynne prepared the chicken and Josh made the salad dressing and steamed the broccoli. They chattered on as they worked, discussing everything from the Latin American debt crisis to the latest cause célèbre of the publishing business.

Over the meal the conversation continued to be light and freewheeling, and they topped off their dinner with cups of espresso and snifters of brandy. Before eiher of them knew it, it was after eleven.

"I'd better get you home," Josh said. "We've both got an early morning tomorrow. And I wouldn't want to take advantage of you by making you stay out too late."

"You mean you wouldn't want to put yourself at a disadvantage by staying out past your bedtime," Lynne countered.

"Ha!" Josh exclaimed skeptically as he took Lynne's coat from the closet and tossed it to her.

On the short walk to her apartment they were silent, each lost in their own thoughts on the quiet, nearly deserted streets. They passed a few people walking dogs and a pair of late-night joggers. Occasionally one of their shoes crunched a dry leaf fallen from one of the few trees on the city's streets. When they reached her building, Lynne pulled her keys from her purse.

"See you in the morning," she said.

"In court," Josh said, taking the keys from her. "I'm glad I ran into you tonight, Lynnie. It was fun. We should do this more often."

"Maybe one night next week, except come to my place."

"Sounds good." He held up the bunch of keys and Lynne pointed out the one that opened the front door. He inserted it, held the door for her and followed her into the vestibule.

"G'night," Lynne said, holding out her hand for the keys.

"G'night." Josh planted a noisy kiss on her cheek, gave her shoulders a tight squeeze and turned to go.

Lynne had pushed open the inner door and was about to enter the building when she suddenly remembered the retirement dinner. "Josh," she called softly, mindful of the first-floor tenants. "Wait a minute."

"Yeah?"

"I should have asked you this earlier, but I completely forgot. I'm in kind of a bind." She explained about the dinner-dance. "Think you can go with me?"

"Are you kidding? Would I miss a chance to wear my tuxedo?"

Lynne stifled a giggle. "You have your own tuxedo?"

"A graduation present from a very proper, very wealthy uncle who thinks no young man can be properly dressed in, as my Uncle Alex says, 'rented finery.'" He pronounced the words as if they signaled at the very least the downfall of Western civilization. "Besides, I love to dance." He swept Lynne into his arms and began to whirl her around the tiny vestibule. "'Dancing in the dark,'" he crooned loudly.

"Josh! The neighbors," Lynne admonished with a giggle. But even in the tiny space she couldn't help but notice that he had some very smooth dancing moves.

He let her go and they said good-night again. Lynne let herself into the building, suddenly feeling very tired but pleasantly so. She mounted the stairs slowly, humming to herself the same tune that Josh had been singing and running through the events of the evening in her mind, playing out each scene as if it were so many frames of a film. It was a movie, she decided as she let herself into her apartment, that she wouldn't mind watching again. And again. And she wouldn't at all mind if some of the scenes ran longer than they had in the original version.

5

SHE HADN'T BEEN THIS NERVOUS since, since.... She'd never been this nervous, Lynne decided, watching her foot move up and down as if driven by a motor over which she had no control. *Cool it*, she told her twitching toes and got up off the couch. She straightened her robe and set off for another lap around the apartment. She'd started to get ready for the dinner-dance far too early and now she had thirty minutes on her hands with nothing left to do except put on her dress—and pace. *I'll never figure out what made me ask Josh to this shindig,* she thought for the umpteenth time as she circled the living room. *I'm sure he only said yes because he felt sorry for me not having a date.* But then there were those few minutes—seconds really—on the couch in his apartment that night. She could have sworn.... Lynne stopped her thoughts before they went any further. That's the sort of thing, she told herself firmly, that only makes trouble.

"Ouch!" she yelled as she stubbed her slippered toe on the leg of the coffee table. Her cry was echoed in the study by a cowboy in a radio advertisement for a new brand of chewing tobacco. He sang its praises with a series of high-pitched, grating yahoos. "Oh, be quiet," Lynne mumbled querulously.

She stomped through the bedroom into the study

and silenced the cowboy with a wrench of the radio dial. She twisted it until she found a hard-driving rock station—maybe a strong steady beat would release some of the tension. But after two minutes her head was nearly pounding. She switched off the radio and wandered back into the living room where she flopped down on the couch and stared restlessly at her own reflection in the window.

FINISHING HIS LUSTY SHOWER ARIA, Josh stepped out of the tub and toweled off vigorously. He wiped the steam from the mirror and lathered up for an extraclose, extrasmooth shave, then doused himself with his favorite after-shave. In his bedroom, he took his tuxedo from its garment bag, brushed it well and proceeded to dress.

Josh—who often joked that he couldn't carry a tune in the Titanic, much less a bucket—confined his lung-expanding vocalizing to the shower, but as he inserted the collar stays and buttoned up his pleated shirtfront he hummed a tuneless but snappy little song. After only two tries he tied his black tie to his satisfaction and gave it a final jaunty twist. For some reason he couldn't quite put his finger on, he was feeling extraordinarily happy tonight. He slipped into his dinner jacket and picked up his keys from the dresser, tossing them into the air and catching them behind his back with a flourish.

NOW THAT SHE had her dress on, Lynne didn't want to sit down for fear of wrinkling it. Her limbs felt numb and tingly at the same time, a sensation she thought would increase with any movement. So she stood stock-still in her study, her hand ready to push the buzzer the second Josh rang. The room hummed with a silence broken only by the woodpeckerlike clatter of Lynne's chattering teeth.

JOSH WALKED THE FEW BLOCKS to Lynne's apartment, savoring the brisk fall air, and as he passed the row of brownstones at the far end of Lynne's block he caught the smell of a wood fire. The smoky aroma made the air almost intoxicating. Ah, those lucky few New Yorkers who had working fireplaces in their apartments, he thought, breathing in deeply. When he reached Lynne's building he hailed a taxi and asked the driver to wait while he went upstairs.

After taking a final tug on his tie he pressed on the bell with three short rhythmic strokes and stepped back slightly, expecting at least a minute's wait. He pictured Lynne rushing from the bedroom, not quite ready, and yelling down the stairs to him that she'd be a few minutes more. But the response to the rings was almost immediate. Caught by surprise he had to scramble to push the door open with a flick of his foot. Inside he took the stairs quickly, and by the time he rapped on Lynne's door his heart was beating a cheerful ka-thunk, ka-thunk, ka-thunk.

The door opened very slowly, revealing a sight that speeded up his already rapidly beating heart. Ka-ka-thunk, ka-ka-thunk, ka-ka-thunk. The pumping was so strong it seemed to Josh that he could hear it, as well as feel it. Standing before him was the most gorgeous woman he'd ever seen. She was wearing a brilliant jade-green silk gown, strapless and cut to accentuate every curve of her body. Above it her eyes shone like a pair of enormous emeralds. Her auburn hair was swept up over one ear and secured with a painted ivory comb. The overall effect was exotic, Oriental in flavor. Had he used every fiber of his imagination he could never have fantasized so beautiful, so breathtaking a Lynne.

"Hello," he said, as if meeting her for the first time.

"Josh," she said with a note of question in her voice, as if she had to confirm that the person in the hall was the one she had expected. In his dashing tuxedo Josh looked more like a debonair playboy than the man she knew. Suddenly the nervousness that had been building in her layer by layer like floors of a skyscraper collapsed and disappeared, leaving only a delicious dusting of anticipation.

From behind his back Josh produced a white florist's box. "For you," he murmured with a small bow.

Not for a moment had Lynne expected him to bring her flowers, and her lower lip began to tremble as she took the box and opened it with shaking hands. Nestled in a crush of green tissue paper was a corsage of two small orchids, snowy white with centers of pale delicate rose. "They're lovely, Josh," she breathed. "Thank you."

"My pleasure," he replied. "Shall I pin them on in the hall or can I come in?" he asked with a lopsided grin.

"I'm sorry," Lynne said, moving aside. "I wasn't thinking."

"Neither was I for a moment. I think my brain stopped. You look absolutely, positively terrific." He surveyed her once more from head to toe. "Simply gorgeous," he added in a taut whisper as he passed by her and stepped into the room.

Just Friends 71

Lynne closed the door behind them and turned to Josh. "Thank you," she said, feeling both pleased and excited. "I guess it does beat shorts and a sweaty T-shirt."

"Hands down," Josh said emphatically. He reached out for the box she held in her right hand. "May I?"

Lynne relinquished the box; Josh lifted the flowers out gently and dropped the empty container on the chair behind him. He took a step toward her and held the corsage up to pin it on, but his hands stopped in midair. "Um, where, uh...I think you're going to have to help me with this," he said uncomfortably, staring at her strapless shoulders.

Lynne looked down at her bare skin and then at Josh. A gale-force laugh ripped through her. "Oh, Josh! I'm sorry, but the look on your face...."

"'My Most Embarrassing Moment.' An essay by Joshua Simmons. It all started one night.... Etcetera, etcetera." Josh took a deep breath and chuckled gamely at himself.

"May I wear the flowers in my hair? I'd like that."

"So would I."

"I'll be right back." Lynne took the corsage from him and went into the bedroom. She removed the comb from her hair and secured the flowers in its place with two bobby pins. "Is this okay?" she asked as she stepped back into the study.

"No," he said quickly. The flowers added a touch of grace and freshness that enhanced her beauty. "It's not just okay. It's...it's—" Josh's tongue tripped over a dozen words in that many seconds, but none seemed right. "It's uh, oh, so okay," he finally said. On the tail of his words came an angry horn blast from outside. He had completely forgotten about the taxi. "Your carriage awaits—but not too patiently," he explained to Lynne.

"I'll just get my wrap." She had borrowed a black velvet evening cape lined with pale yellow satin from her sister-in-law. She handed it to Josh and he draped it over her shoulders. They flew downstairs and into the waiting cab.

JOSH AND LYNNE'S TAXI drew up beside the flock of black limousines huddled in front of the Hotel de Georges on Fifth Avenue. A green-and-gold-uniformed doorman stepped quickly off the curb to open the door and help Lynne out of the cab. Josh paid the driver and offered Lynne his arm.

Another uniformed doorman held open the ornate brass door of the hotel and they glided into the lobby, sinking into the plush carpet as if it were sand on a beach. From overhead an elaborate crystal chandelier bestowed soft understated light. Though the lobby was full of guests and employees, there was a stately quiet; the only sounds were of hushed voices and rustling fabric.

"It's not exactly the Apollo," Josh whispered as they mounted the imposing staircase, "but it'll do."

Lynne stifled an unseemly giggle and nudged Josh gently in the ribs. He put his free hand on the arm that was linked through his and squeezed it lightly. A swift jolt of excitement passed through her at his touch and she had to control yet another impulse to giggle aloud.

At the top of the stairs a tuxedoed floor manager appeared before them unasked and pointed the way to the elevators that led to the ballroom. The elevator whisked them up one floor and they stepped into a crowded anteroom. As they waited to check Lynne's wrap, Josh pointed discreetly into the center of the crowd. "Isn't that Lilian Mason?" The retired screen star was one of Josh's all-time favorite actresses.

Lynne nodded. "Alan edited her autobiography."

"She's still gorgeous, isn't she?" Unlike many stars of her generation, Lilian Mason hadn't tried to disguise her age. Her hair was silvery gray; the lines in her face had not been obliterated by surgical means. Her skin and eyes glowed with vim and vitality. "I'd love to meet her," Josh said wistfully.

"Come on, then. I'll introduce you."

"Very funny, Farrell."

"No joke, Josh. I was Alan's assistant when we published her book." Lynne took his hand and pulled him through the crowd to the cluster of people surrounding Lilian Mason. "I hope she remembers me," Lynne muttered under her breath.

"Hello, Miss Mason," she said when the group ahead of them had moved away. The bright blue eyes looked blank for a split second and Lynne was about to remind Miss Mason who she was when the firm mouth widened into a welcoming smile.

"Lynne, dear. So nice to see you again. I can see you didn't think I'd remember you, but I'm not as quick with names as I used to be. You're looking charming, dear. Quite charming." She shook Lynne's hand warmly. "And who is this handsome fellow? I've never seen him before," she said flirtatiously.

Lynne introduced a blushing Josh who stammered a hello and seemed about to say something else.

"Now Mr. Simmons," Lilian Mason interrupted, "you look like a man who is about to say something he'll want to kick himself in the head for later. Believe me, it's not necessary, dear. I've heard it all."

Josh laughed sheepishly. "You're absolutely right, Miss Mason."

"At my age one has that privilege."

Lilian Mason chatted with them for another few minutes and then moved graciously on to another couple waiting to talk with her.

"That's it," Josh said as they threaded their way to the ballroom entrance. "I can die a happy man now."

"Not yet you can't. The evening is just beginning."

"And I've got a feeling it can only get better." Josh beamed at her. Lynne shivered happily.

At the door Lynne gave her name to the hostess. "You and Mr. Simmons are at table twelve, Miss Farrell," she said and pointed to its location on the room plan before her. Lynne thanked her and they joined the people waiting to greet the guest of honor in the receiving line.

The line moved quickly and Lynne was welcomed effusively by Alan Parker and his wife. The staid Sam Hamilton, president of the company, with whom she had a more-distant relationship, gave her a reserved but nonetheless warm welcome, and invited them to get a drink from the bar at the far end of the room.

"I never expected anything this elaborate," Josh said as they crossed the huge two-story-high room. The enormous windows that looked out over Fifth Avenue were draped in heavy gold-fringed brocade, held back by tasseled swags. At the front of the room a raised dais held the tables for the guests of honor.

Just Friends 75

The floor was covered with scores of round tables, all bearing immaculate white linen cloths and centerpieces of rust, yellow and white asters and mums. At the back of the room there was a parquet dance floor and a slightly raised stage where chairs and music stands were set up for the band that would undoubtedly play after the meal.

Josh made it through the crush at the bar and returned to Lynne bearing two glasses of ice-cold champagne. They found an unoccupied corner at the edge of the dance floor and raised their glasses to each other. "To champagne and dressing up and beautiful ladies who know Lilian Mason," Josh propped.

Blushing slightly, Lynne acknowledged the toast and took a sip of the pale gold wine. It slipped smoothly over her tongue, making her whole mouth tingle. A waiter came by with a silver tray of canapés. Lynne selected a toast point covered with caviar and chopped egg, and Josh chose the same. They nibbled daintily on the delectable delicacy and then bathed away the tart salty taste with more sweet icy champagne.

"Now I know what it means to be as happy as a pig in mud. I could wallow in this stuff all night." Josh took another healthy sip of champagne and drained his glass. "Drink up, Lynnie. I have a feeling we haven't even made a dent in our champagne allowance." He grabbed her hand and pulled her back toward the bar.

While Josh was getting their glasses refilled, Lynne spotted one of her fellow editors, whose husband was also lined up at the bar. When the men returned the four of them chatted, Lynne and her colleague pointing out the celebrities who had come to honor one of the publishing world's most well-respected figures. Besides Lilian Mason there was a former New York State governor, a popular Soviet émigré writer and the theater critic for a national news magazine.

Lynne felt a thrill just looking around the room. It was alive with the colors of hundreds of splendid gowns the sounds of voices raised in conversation. Out of the corner of her eye she glanced at Josh and unexpectedly met his simultaneous sideways look at her; he winked and grinned broadly. Lynne looked away quickly. Josh's deep dark eyes were doing something strange to her tonight. Every time she looked at him she felt giddy. Maybe it was the champagne and the heady atmosphere. Whatever it was, she made up her mind to enjoy it.

The staff had closed the doors to the ballroom and the receiving line had broken up. Waiters with bottles of champagne were circulating to fill empty glasses, and the talk and laughter grew to sforzando until the sound in the room was like that in a concert hall during the climax of a symphony—except that the climax was sustained with no diminuendo. Though she and Josh were standing shoulder to shoulder, Lynne had to speak more loudly to make herself heard above the din.

Gradually she became aware of one voice predominating over the others and realized that Sam Hamilton was at the microphone on the dais asking people to take their places. It took several minutes for everyone to be seated, but when they were a parade of white-coated waiters marched out from the kitchen to begin serving.

The meal began with a subtle cream of sorrel soup

and continued with a tricolor salmon, scallop and spinach pâté. The main course was medallions of beef in a bordelaise sauce accompanied by tiny roasted potatoes and carrots in a butter-and-parsley sauce. Each course was served with a different wine and it took nearly two hours for the guests to consume the delicious meal. The symphonic din that had prevailed during the cocktail hour had disappeared, replaced by a chamber ensemble of conversation and clinking china, silver and crystal. Because conversing across the large tables was difficult, while they were eating, Lynne and Josh talked quietly to their immediate neighbors or to each other.

As the meal progressed, both found they had less and less to say to the people around them, not because the others were uninteresting, but because they were finding each other more compelling than ever. With their heads close together, talking in tones only they could hear, they could have been alone in a small bistro, not in the grand ballroom of a magnificent hotel surrounded by hundreds of other people.

When the last dishes had been cleared away, Sam Hamilton proposed the evening's official toast to the guest of honor. A short round of speeches followed, bearing testimony to Alan Parker's distinguished career. When the speakers concluded, Alan rose to say a few words.

"The most important thing I've made in my career has not been money. Everyone knows there's no money in publishing...." At this the crowd chuckled appreciatively, and he waited for the room to quiet down. "Nor has it been books, of which I've made quite a few...and one or two of them were even good." This garnered another laugh from the crowd and Alan quieted them with a wave of his hand. "No," he continued, "the most important thing I've made in my career has been friends."

Lynne felt Josh's hand steal under the table and find hers. He gave it a hearty squeeze and he and Lynne exchanged an affirming smile. But as Alan spoke, Lynne felt her palm grow hot in Josh's. Almost imperceptibly at first, he began to stroke the back of her hand with his thumb, creating little spots of intense white heat wherever he touched. Lynne continued to hear Alan's words, but they stopped registering in her brain. The thunderclap of applause that followed Alan's speech brought her concentration crashing back, and she snatched her hand from Josh's and jumped to her feet to join the crowd in a standing ovation.

When the applause tapered off, the band struck up a waltz and Alan led his wife down from the dais and through the still-standing crowd, across the room onto the dance floor. After the first chorus other couples from nearby tables joined in and Josh leaned over and whispered to Lynne.

In a matter of seconds she was in his arms being whirled around the dance floor. It seemed as if there were a cushion of air beneath her feet, for they seemed never to come into contact with the floor. Josh was a wonderful dancer, light on his feet, but a strong unhesitant partner. Lynne had never thought herself anything more than an average dancer, but Josh's lead was so easy to follow that she began to smoothly perform combinations that would have had her tripping over her own feet with a less-competent partner. The waltz was followed by a foxtrot, and after that a rumba. Josh kept her on the floor for all three and she practically had to pull him away after the third dance for a break.

"If you won't dance, you must drink some champagne," Josh said, guiding her toward the bar.

"Anything, as long as I don't have to dance for a few minutes," Lynne said between breaths. "Where did you learn to dance like that?"

Josh fingered the lapel of his dinner jacket. "Remember Uncle Alex of the tuxedo? I used to visit him during the summer and he'd give me lessons. Then I'd get to practice at his parties. He thought it was barbaric that young people weren't taught to dance properly. When I was twelve it embarrassed the heck out of me, but as I got older I began to see the advantages." He flashed her a devilish smile. "I don't mind dazzling the dames now and then, kid."

"That was the worst Humphrey Bogart imitation I've ever heard," Lynne said with a giggle.

Josh shrugged complacently. "Well, you can't be good at everything, can you?"

The bar was less crowded now with people dancing and milling about the room, visiting from table to table, and Josh was back at her side with a glass of champagne in seconds. But they didn't stand on the sidelines long. When the band began to beat out a spirited lindy hop, Josh couldn't resist dancing. He took the glass from Lynne's hand and swept her off to the dance floor.

She missed Josh's complicated behind-the-back passes the first couple of times, but then caught on to the move; the last time she added a tricky step of her own, which caused Josh to let out a whoop of pleasure. That turned a few heads and made them the object of some attention during the band's last chorus. Some of the applause that followed the music was directed toward them, which delighted Josh and made Lynne bashful, especially when Josh twirled her around and pulled her into a dramatic close clinch.

But the music started again, this time a romantic ballad. Lynne hardly thought Josh could have pulled her any closer, but he did. She could feel his breath in her ear as he piloted her gently in a small circle. He tightened his grip around her waist and leaned his cheek against hers.

"I'm having a wonderful time, Lynnie," he whispered.

"Josh," she breathed, and relaxed into his arms. Maybe it was the music, maybe it was the wine, or perhaps the exertion of dancing, but Lynne felt limp, as if all her bones were made of some quivering gelatinous material. She felt so languid that if Josh had not been holding her up she might have floated to the floor. But she felt his strong arms, his sturdy body supporting her, and she relied on him as she knew she could.

"I should have taken you dancing a long time ago," he murmured.

"I wish you had," she whispered, resting her head on his shoulder.

The dance seemed to go on forever—Lynne ceased to have any sense of time passing at all—and yet it was over far too soon. Josh did not release her when the music stopped, but continued to hold her, pressing her to him and stroking her hair in tempo to music only they could hear.

The band was several beats into a spirited cha-cha

Harlequin Temptation

Have you ever thought
you were in love
with one man...only
to feel attracted to another?

That's just one of the temptations you'll find facing the women in *Harlequin Temptation* romance novels.

Sensuous ... contemporary ... compelling ... reflecting today's love relationships!

The passionate torment of a woman torn between two loves...the siren call of a career...the magnetic advances of an impetuous employer—nothing is left unexplored in this romantic series from Harlequin. You'll thrill to a candid new frankness as men and women seek to form lasting relationships in the face of temptations that threaten true love. *Don't miss a single one!* You can start *Harlequin Temptation* coming to *your* home each month for just $1.75 per book. Begin with your FREE copy of *First Impressions*.

Mail the reply card today!

GET THIS BOOK FREE!

First Impressions
by Maris Soule

He was involved with her best friend! Tracy Dexter couldn't deny her attraction to her new boss. Mark Prescott looked more like a jet set playboy than a high school principal—and he acted like one, too. It wasn't right for Tracy to go out with him, not when her friend Rose had already staked a claim. It wasn't right, even though Mark's eyes were so persuasive, his kiss so probing and intense. Even though his hands scorched her body with a teasing, raging fire...and when he gently lowered her to the floor she couldn't find the words to say no.

A word of warning to our regular readers: While Harlequin books are always in good taste, you'll find more sensuous writing in *Harlequin Temptation* than in other Harlequin romance series.

® ™ Trademarks of Harlequin Enterprises Ltd.

Exclusive Harlequin home subscriber benefits!
- CONVENIENCE of home delivery
- NO CHARGE for postage and handling
- FREE *Harlequin Romance Digest*®
- FREE BONUS books
- NEW TITLES 2 months ahead of retail
- A MEMBER of the largest romance fiction book club in the world

GET FIRST IMPRESSIONS FREE AS YOUR INTRODUCTION TO *Harlequin Temptation* ™ PLUS A FREE TOTE BAG!

® No one touches the heart of a woman quite like Harlequin

YES, please send me FREE and **without obligation** my *Harlequin Temptation* romance novel, *First Impressions* and my FREE tote bag. If you do not hear from me after I have examined my FREE book, please send me 4 new *Harlequin Temptation* novels each month as soon as they come off the press. I understand that I will be billed only $1.75 per book (total $7.00). There are no shipping and handling or any other hidden charges. There is no minimum number of books that I have to purchase. In fact, I may cancel this arrangement at any time. The FREE tote bag and *First Impressions* are mine to keep as a free gift, even if I do not buy any additional books.   142 CIX MDF3

Name

Address   Apt. No.

City   State/Prov.   Zip/Postal Code

Signature (If under 18, parent or guardian must sign.)

This offer is limited to one order per household and not valid to present *Harlequin Temptation* subscribers. We reserve the right to exercise discretion in granting membership.

PRINTED IN U.S.A.

Get this romance novel and tote bag FREE as your introduction to

Harlequin Temptation ™

See exciting details inside.

BUSINESS REPLY CARD

First Class Permit No. 70 Tempe, AZ

POSTAGE WILL BE PAID BY ADDRESSEE

Harlequin Reader Service®
2504 West Southern Avenue
Tempe, Arizona 85282

NO POSTAGE
NECESSARY
IF MAILED
IN THE
UNITED STATES

when Josh pulled away from her and stepped into the one-two, one-two-three movement. Lynne followed him, and after a few moments the insistent beat drove away all the languor and tenderness of the previous magical dance and replaced it with a joy and zest that seemed like a palpable force, something she could reach out and touch. Looking at Josh, she knew he was feeling something similar, and they danced to the Latin beat with a Latin sense of abandon.

Lynne was so absorbed in the dance that she heard only the tail end of Alan Parker's sentence. When she finally saw his outstretched arms, she realized he wanted to cut in. It took her another second to register the fact that his partner was Lilian Mason. Josh was grinning so widely that his smile seemed almost to cut his face in two. Without missing a beat, he took the famous screen star into his arms, and Lynne was left with Alan.

"Your young man cuts quite a rug, as we used to say. This cutting-in business was all Lilian's idea. Not that I don't want to dance with you myself, but a man with my sense of self-preservation hesitates before cutting in on a man half his age with so, shall we say, definite an interest in a woman. Unless he's the young woman's father."

Lynne felt herself turning an unbecoming beet red.

"I thought blushing had gone completely out of fashion these days," Alan went on with a twinkle in his eye. "But it would appear that I'm wrong. You've been holding out on me, Lynne. I understood from office scuttlebutt that your love life left something to be desired."

"Oh, Josh and I are just friends," Lynne said quickly.

"It's a good thing you're not my daughter, young lady," Alan admonished, "or I'd turn you over my knee. For lying," he added mischievously, "not the other."

Though she didn't think it possible, Lynne turned an even darker red.

"It's a pleasure, Mr. Simmons," Lilian Mason said to Josh, "to see a young man who knows how to dance. Really dance, I mean, not that shaking and bumping that passes for dancing nowadays. Like so many other things, fine ballroom dancing is a dying art."

As they finished the cha-cha Josh told Miss Mason about his Uncle Alex.

"I think I would have liked your uncle."

"And I'm sure he would have liked you." Josh reluctantly relinquished his partner when the music stopped. "This has been a real pleasure, Miss Mason." He inclined his head and bowed slightly from the waist.

"For me, too, Mr. Simmons." Alan and Lynne appeared beside them and Miss Mason turned to Alan. "If you will be so kind as to get my wrap, Alan, I think it's time for me to get these old bones back home. Good evening."

As Alan and Lilian Mason retreated, all Josh could do was shake his head and mutter, "Wow," over and over. Finally he looked up at Lynne. "Pinch me," he said, "hard."

Lynne squeezed his cheek between her thumb and forefinger. "Honestly, Josh, you sound like a little boy who's just seen Superman leap a tall building in a mighty bound."

"It was better than that, Lynnie. Wow," he said again. "Would you mind sitting out the next dance? I need to take a break and recover."

"I thought you'd never ask," Lynne replied, still reeling slightly from her conversation with Alan.

They got soft drinks from the bar and sat on the sidelines until the bandleader announced the final set of the evening.

Josh stole a glance at his watch. "Guess how long we've been dancing," he said.

"An hour or so?" Lynne ventured.

"Wrong. Almost three hours." The music started and Josh pulled her to her feet. "Come on, let's not waste a single beat."

And they didn't. The last set of dances flew by. The longer they danced the longer Lynne felt she could go on. She never wanted the music to stop, but finally the last dance of the evening was announced.

It was another slow ballad, and before Josh took her in his arms for it he said, "I hope this won't be our last dance."

"How could it be?" Lynne said lightly, belying the heavy beating of her heart. She stepped into his arms and felt them wrap securely around her. Barely daring to breathe for fear of bursting the clear protective bubble that seemed to surround them, Lynne leaned into the dance.

She had never experienced movement that could be called sweet before, but that's what this dance was like—a light feathery meringue, almost unbearably sweet. It was not a dance one could make a steady diet of, but one in which the taste, and the memory of the taste, lingers long after it is over. Lynne savored every precious morsel of it, sensing in Josh's touch that it was not the end of the feast, but only the beginning.

6

THE COLD AIR OUTSIDE the hotel hit Lynne like the slap of a wave on the beach. It was playful and invigorating. She took in a long reviving breath and felt the flush start to drain out of her dance-rosied cheeks. The doorman jumped ahead to hail them a cab, but Josh, after getting a nod from Lynne, waved him away. "We'll walk, thank you." The doorman gave them a look that said they were only one pair of the crazy people he dealt with every day. Josh and Lynne didn't look at each other so as to keep from laughing, and Josh draped a protective arm around Lynne's shoulders and piloted her down Fifth Avenue.

"I thought I might mention that we're going the wrong way," Lynne said, giggles escaping like fireflies into the night. She pointed her thumb behind her with a couple of quick jabs. "Uptown's thataway, pard."

"But I bet you've never seen Fifth Avenue at—" Josh lifted his sleeve and glanced at his watch "—almost four in the morning."

The street was deserted; only an occasional cab or car whizzed past them. Across the avenue, beyond the stone wall that surrounded Central Park, the dark silhouettes of trees stabbed the night sky, their few remaining leaves dangling in defiance of fall winds and the winter that was stealing closer day by day. Lynne shivered slightly and Josh pulled her closer to him.

"It's like being on a movie set after the shooting is over," Lynne whispered. "I don't want to talk too loudly. Don't want to wake up the guard and have him come and tell us to go away."

"There's no one else here," Josh whispered back. "We've got the whole place to ourselves, as if we owned it." They had just crossed Fifty-ninth Street. The Plaza Hotel, a few lights staring unexpectedly from its many windows, stood stately and serene behind the fountain in the small plaza from which it derived its name. "Our personal guest house," Josh said with a sweeping gesture toward the majestic old hotel. "And the annex." He pointed back at the Sherry-Netherland.

"Wouldn't that be something?" Lynne said in a low longing tone.

"No wouldn'ts about it. Tonight we can have anything we want." He stopped walking and brought her around to face him. His hand caressed her chin gently.

"Anything?" Lynne asked shakily.

"Anything," he repeated in a husky whisper as he brought his face close to hers. His lips grazed her cheek and settled lightly on her mouth. His arms moved under her cape and surrounded her. Lynne felt her head begin to spin and put her hands on his arms to steady herself. Suddenly he clasped her tightly to him and kissed her deeply, avidly, fervently.

Her first taste of Josh's passion was strange, like the first taste of a tropical fruit she had long known about but never before encountered. It was nothing like she would have imagined, and it was nothing like anything she had tasted before. It was sweet but substantial; filling but so tantalizing that she had to ask for more. Her grip on Josh's arms tightened and their kiss became more ardent.

"Lynnie, oh, Lynnie," Josh breathed, gently breaking away from her and cradling her head on his shoulder. "It's heady stuff, this owning a city," he said, stroking her hair.

Her own head felt as if she had been standing in a bell tower while the bells were pealing wildly. Even though they had stopped, there was a ringing echo in her brain that made Josh's words sound muffled and distant despite the fact that his mouth was just inches from her ear. "You'd better hold on to me, Josh. I feel a little tipsy," Lynne said. Her own voice seemed to come from far away, too.

"Hold on to you? I don't know if I'll ever let you go." His arms surrounded her with an almost crushing force, and his mouth came down on hers in a kiss that set off a new round of ringing in her ears. "I'd like to take you home, Lynnie, take us home," he whispered as he lifted his lips from hers.

She tried to speak, but her throat was so full of emotion the words could not get through. But Josh saw the answer in her eyes and laid his lips gently on her forehead. Quickly he slipped one arm out from behind her back and stuck two fingers between his teeth. A piercing whistle shattered the late-night quiet, and a taxi careened around a corner and screeched to a stop in front of them.

With a click of his heels, Josh opened the door and helped her into the cab. They sat silently, holding hands, their fingers playing the prelude to a symphony that was yet to be composed. Lynne's heart was beating so fast that she hardly felt the jumping and jolting of the taxi, and when the driver slammed to a halt in front of her building she had the sensation she was still moving.

Josh took the keys from her and let them into the building. Every creak the old steps made sounded to Lynne like volcanic rumblings; the snap of the bolts in the locks on her door like rocks being split. Every sense was throbbing, a thousand times more sensitive than ever before.

Josh pushed open the apartment door and took one of Lynne's hands in his. He pressed her keys into it. "I can go now, Lynnie, but once I step through that door—"

Lynne silenced him with a finger on his lips. "We're home, Josh," she said simply, realizing that she had waited for this moment for weeks. Since that day in the park when Josh had—

"Penny for your thoughts," Josh murmured, guiding her inside and closing the door behind them. Because Lynne disliked coming home to a dark apartment she always left one lamp burning when she went out at night. In its dim light their figures cast long shadows across the floor.

"I was just thinking of the day we had breakfast in the park and you made that sailboat...."

Josh took her in his arms and began to dance her slowly around the room. "'I give to you and you give to me....'"

Though the tune he sang only vaguely resembled the song as she knew it, Lynne felt as rapturous as if she was being serenaded by Pavarotti himself. "'True love, true love,'" she joined in softly.

Just Friends 89

Josh slipped the cape from her shoulders, let it drop on her reading chair as they passed it, and continued to dance her toward the nearest door.

"That's the kitchen, Josh," Lynne whispered.

He did a quick about-face. "I'm hungry, but not for anything that's in there." He began to nibble enticingly on her earlobe. "Will I find what I want through that other door?"

"Let's put it this way," Lynne said with a playful grin, "you won't find a tiger."

"Just a lady?" he asked lasciviously.

Even as they spoke, Lynne wondered how they could joke at a moment like this. But she and Josh always joked with each other. Why should this moment be so different? Was it not another pearl to be threaded onto the string they had already begun?

Josh's voice turned serious, raspy. "A lovely, lovely lady." He stopped at the door to her bedroom and kissed her fully, his hands ranging up and down her bare arms and across her bare shoulders. Lynne shuddered with delight. "Come, lovely." He took her by the hand and led her into the room.

By the side of the bed he stopped. "Turn around," he whispered. She turned her back toward him and he nuzzled her neck. One hand strayed to the zipper of her gown and he inched it down slowly past her waist. Lynne felt the bodice of the dress open and slip down to rest on her hips. Josh's lips moved down her spine and he reached around to caress her freed breasts. Lynne gasped at the sensation of fingers that were burning hot and ice-cold at the same time. Her nipples grew stiff under his touch.

Still kissing her back, Josh dropped his hands to her hips and eased the dress down. "Step out of this," he whispered. "It's too beautiful to crush." He held her hand to steady her as she stepped clear of the dress.

Josh turned her around slowly. "Lovely," he said hoarsely. "Like a woman in a painting by Gauguin." He kissed each breast lightly. "But without the tan, of course." Josh bent down and picked up her dress.

"You can just lay it across the chair, Josh." She felt free and unselfconscious, even though she was half-naked, and watched Josh as he placed the dress carefully over the back of the chair near the bed and slipped out of his jacket. He lined up the shoulders and folded it in half, placing it on the seat of the chair. He reached for his tie, but Lynne stopped him.

"Let me," she said, "please." She tugged on the end of the tie and the knot unfurled. She slipped it from under his collar and went to work on the buttons of his shirt, undoing them slowly. Josh's breathing increased as she released each button. His chest moved in and out rapidly as she kissed the spots she revealed. She pulled the shirt down over his shoulders and tossed it and the tie on her dressing table.

Josh pressed her to him roughly, and their naked skins met for the first time. His chest was warm and dry, with the strength of a sun-drenched rock. How good it felt to be held by someone she knew and trusted—and wanted. Lynne clung to him until Josh gently disengaged himself from their embrace.

He placed his hands on her hips and drew down the long half-slip, leaving her in her real silk stockings, panties and high heels. Josh sat her on the edge of the bed and she kicked off her shoes. He knelt beside her and let his hands move slowly up the length of her legs. He unhooked one delicate transparent stocking and rolled it down her leg centimeter by centimeter, his mouth following the silk, replacing the warmth of the fabric with the heat of his kisses. Weak, almost feeble with desire, Lynne fell back on the bed.

He shucked the rest of his clothes in a couple of swift motions and joined her. "You look incredibly sexy like that," he said, stretching out beside her and propping himself up on one elbow. With his other hand he reached up and carefully drew the orchids from her hair. He caressed her with the flowers, passing the soft petals over her face, her breasts, her belly. Using the flower to toy with the insides of her thighs, he bent his head and licked at her nipples. Lynne stiffened with pleasure and did not relax even when he withdrew his tongue.

Josh rose to his knees and straddled Lynne's legs. The corsage floated from his hands to the floor beside the bed, and his fingers cruised lazily from her shoulders to the tops of her panties. He tugged at them, but stopped to bend down and bury his face between her breasts. With a deep groan he sat up and whisked off the panties and the garter belt under them, leaving her utterly exposed. Josh gazed at her for a long moment, then covered her body with his and rolled them onto their sides.

"I've been wanting to do this for so long. I just didn't realize it until we were standing there in front of the hotel. Lynnie, Lynnie, my lovely Lynnie," he whispered in her ear. "If you only knew how much I want you."

"Show me, Josh. Show me."

He gave her an achingly deep kiss; he nuzzled, he caressed, he fondled every inch of her body. With every touch she grew tauter and more pliant, stronger with wanting and weaker with desire. Just at the moment when she could no longer bear the waiting, Josh rolled them over and poised above her.

He slipped inside of her slowly and easily. Lynne let out a soft cry of contentment. The unsettled feeling that had nagged at her since Josh had returned from his vacation flowed out of her like an ebbing tide. She'd only enjoyed this new contentment for a moment when a new tide, forceful and insistent, rolled back in on her unexpectedly, like a sudden squall at sea. She tightened her grip on Josh's back. He cried out and plunged more deeply inside her. The tide threatened to spill over and engulf her. She tried to hold it back, but suddenly she was drowning in sensation—wet, wild, wanton sensation.

Feeling her begin to shudder, Josh slid his hands beneath her buttocks and crushed her to him, forcing her to ride the wave until it crashed onto the shore, knocking the breath out of her. Gasping, she clutched at his back, weakened and spent. "Easy, take it easy," he whispered, all the while daubing her face with soothing kisses.

He waited until her breathing had quieted down, and began to rock gently inside her. He felt her open herself to him, an invitation to take as much pleasure as he had given her. He accepted and took his time with her, enjoying her, wanting to make this last forever. But even though he stretched his motions out, willing himself to go slowly, carefully, his breaths began to come faster and faster, each one starting in a place deeper down inside him.

When his breathing began to feel as if it started simultaneously in his head and his toes, Josh knew he couldn't hold back much longer. He closed his eyes and took himself as far into her as he could. Just as he thought he had reached the place he wanted, she opened further to him. A ragged breath wracked his body, ripping through it like a tornado. He stiffened, suspended in a swirling whirling world. It stopped spinning for a moment and then he tumbled down, down, down into Lynne, into the most incredible softness and sweetness he had ever felt.

He lay heavily upon her, his head nestled on her shoulder. Her warm hands caressed his back and she made little cooing noises in his ear. A great happiness welled up in Josh, and a laugh bubbled out of him.

"What's so funny?" Lynne whispered.

He propped himself up on one elbow. "What a couple of dummies we are," he murmured, tracing her kiss-swollen mouth with a fingertip. "Those trees sure fooled us."

"What trees?"

"The ones we were looking at that made us miss the forest." Josh rolled over and pulled Lynne to him, her head resting on his chest.

"Silly," she whispered, reaching up to stroke his cheek.

He took her hand and held it over his still rapidly beating heart. They lay quietly together. Lovemaking, dancing and champagne had lowered their guard and sleep quickly stole in to keep them for what little was left of the darkness.

LYNNE WOKE several hours later. Squinting at the bedside clock out of one eye she saw that it was just after ten in the morning. Her mouth was as dry as a desert and her head ached slightly. She raised herself up and leaned back against the headboard. Seeing Josh sleeping next to her brought back the events of the night before like a film running at double speed. It made her feel dizzy and she let out a small sigh.

Josh stirred and rolled over onto his side. One hand crept from beneath the covers and landed on Lynne's leg. "G'morning," he murmured without opening his eyes.

"Hello," she murmured softly.

"Don't shout," Josh said, raising his head off the pillow and giving her a rueful grin. "Think I had too much champagne last night." He licked his dry lips.

"Want some juice?"

"Mmm."

Lynne made her way unsteadily to the kitchen. It was chilly in the apartment and the cool air cleared her head and quickened her step as she returned to the bedroom with two large glasses of orange juice. She hurried back under the covers.

Josh propped himself up in bed and downed his juice almost in one gulp. "Just what the doctor ordered," he said, putting his empty glass on the bedside table.

Lynne sipped hers more slowly, aware that Josh's eyes were on her. She finished her juice with short quick gulps and when she put the glass down Josh said hoarsely, "Come here." He patted the mattress beside him and held out his arms. Lynne snuggled up to him and he pulled them both down under the covers.

"You feel good," he whispered. His mouth found hers and soon his cool, orange-scented lips were pressing hard against hers, his tongue exploring the inside of her willing mouth.

They made love swiftly and urgently, with none of the prolonged preliminaries of the night before. This time it was as if someone had ignited a firecracker with a short fuse. The match of passion hardly had touched them before they were ablaze with feeling and moving toward a crackling climax.

"Josh," Lynne cried, certain that she would be shattered into a thousand tiny pieces. "Hold me." His grip tightened and she exploded in his arms. In the aftershock she felt him burst inside her. He called her name and collapsed heavily atop her. But she did not mind the weight. It was like a comforting blanket—warm and safe after a long trek in a snow-covered wilderness.

THE NEXT TIME LYNNE WOKE it was midafternoon. Josh lay beside her, his hair tousled, his breathing light. She knew his face so well, and yet he could have been a stranger, someone she'd met only the night before.... Just the thought of it made Lynne's toes curl. The man lying next to her was no longer just her friend—he was her lover, and she was his.

Lynne drew in a deep breath as the significance of this thought began to work its way through her brain. Needing a moment alone to think, she stroked his cheek and eased herself out of bed so she wouldn't wake him. She took her robe from the hook inside the closet door and went into the kitchen to make some coffee, stopping in the bathroom on the way to freshen up.

Teeth brushed, face washed, hair combed, Lynne stepped into the kitchen. She took the kettle from the stove and filled it, ground some coffee beans and put a fresh filter in the top half of the pot. Perched on the kitchen stool, she waited for the kettle to whistle. Her body felt full and heavy with sleep and love, but there was also a strange mass of feeling, like a glowing ball, in the pit of her stomach. It was part excitement, part nervous anticipation of what would come next. Her old relationship with Josh was clearly over, but what would the new one be like? The ball of feeling suddenly became heavier, leaden, and a wave of foreboding assailed her. She should have sent him home last night. Starting an affair with Josh had been crazy, impetuous—and the most exhilarating thing she had ever done.

As the kettle began to whistle, she hopped off the stool and lifted the water from the burner, hoping the noise had not awakened Josh. She needed a few minutes alone to sort out her contradictory emotions. She poured the boiling water over the ground beans, and the aroma of coffee filled the small kitchen. Steaming mug of coffee in hand, Lynne again perched on the stool. Her thoughts raced around in her head like the atomic particles in high-school chemistry diagrams. Some broke ahead to the future, calling up pictures of other nights, other days with Josh; some jumped nostalgically to their past; but the quickest and strongest leaped about frenetically, crashing and colliding, warning that she and Josh had compromised both the past and the future last night.

Lured by the smell of fresh coffee, Josh struggled out of an unsettled sleep, unable to remember where he was or how he had gotten there. But the moment he managed to open his heavy-lidded eyes it all rushed back to him. The images of dancing, of Lynne, of making love, strung together and hurtled toward him like a speeding train. The dizzying thought passed and he reached out, relieved to find the other side of the bed warm but empty.

He sat up and ran his hands through his matted curls, full consciousness returning. The morning after gripped him pincerlike right between the eyes. Except that it was three in the afternoon, a glance at the bedside clock told him. *What have I done*, he thought with an inward groan. Getting carried away was one thing—but with Lynne? He fully understood why it had happened, but in the light of day he wasn't so sure he should have let it happen.

He heaved himself out of bed and hurried to the door on the other side of the room, assuming it was the bathroom. It was a closet. Damned railroad flats, he thought irritably. The bathrooms are always next to the kitchen. Feeling uncomfortably naked, he wrapped himself in the most readily available cover-up—a bed sheet—and left the room. He found Lynne sitting on a stool in her cramped kitchen, wearing a blue quilted robe, looking fresh but quite pensive as she stared into her coffee mug. She hadn't heard him approach. "G'morning," he said gruffly.

Lynne looked up sharply to see Josh with one of her flowered sheets draped toga-style around his body. "Planning on addressing the Roman forum?" she asked with an ill-suppressed smile. From the look on his face she could see that Josh was not amused by her comment. She wiped the smile away.

"I figured it was this or modeling some of your lingerie." Aware of how foolish he looked, Josh pointed to the door at the back of the kitchen. "Um, is that where you've hidden the bathroom?"

"I had nothing to do with it," she answered testily. "Blame the clever people who installed the plumbing." She stopped herself from saying anything else. No sense in making a bad start worse.

"Very convenient," Josh commented dryly.

"Clean towels are on the shelf," she said, hurrying to put the coffee things on a tray and give him some privacy. "I have a terry-cloth robe in the closet. I'll leave it outside the door." *Why*, she asked herself as she went to get the robe, *doesn't anyone think of the morning—or afternoon—after, before rushing into things?*

She left the robe for Josh and went into the study. The room was unnervingly quiet and she turned on the radio and sat at the table, sipping what was left of her coffee.

Josh emerged from the bathroom looking less comical but still not entirely comfortable in her white terry-cloth robe. She poured him a cup of coffee and was about to add cream, but he stopped her, saying, "Don't bother, I'll do it myself." He added cream and sugar and sat down opposite her.

"Would you like something to eat? Some toast? I can scramble some eggs if you'd like."

"Just some toast, please."

While Lynne was in the kitchen, Josh got up and walked around the room, examining the books and records on the shelves, trying to quell his edginess. *Cool it*, he told himself. *This isn't some woman you picked up in a bar last night, it's Lynne.* Which was precisely the problem. In the light of afternoon he didn't know how to behave with her, what to say, what to do. He pulled a record off the shelf at random and began to read the liner notes.

"Anything you'd like to listen to?" Lynne asked brightly, entering the room with a plate of buttered toast and a jar of jam.

"No, the radio's fine." Josh pushed the record back into its slot.

They munched their toast silently, the crunching audible over the music. Lynne jumped up after eating half a piece. "I'll just heat the coffee up," she said.

"Don't bother."

"It's no trouble," she insisted. *This is silly*, she told herself as she waited for the steam to rise from the pot. *I'm acting like he's someone I never met until last night.* She resolved to set things right when she went back to the table.

"I just want you to know, Josh," she said as she poured him a second cup of coffee, "that I'm not sorry about what happened last night...and this morning."

"Neither am I," he said hastily. "I guess...I guess it just takes some getting used to—for both of us." Memories of their lovemaking poured down on him like a sudden summer sun shower. He seized her hand and kissed the palm. "You were lovely last night, Lynnie."

"So were you," she answered shyly.

They finished their coffee slowly, both unsure of what to say or do next. Josh rose first. "I'd like to get back to my place. I suppose.... Would you like to do something later? See a movie or have a meal?" he asked uncertainly.

Had the invitation been less halting Lynne might

have considered it for more than a mere moment. "Thanks, but I have some reading to do tonight. And some sleep to catch up on."

"Me, too," Josh said gratefully. "Pile of reports this high." He indicated its height by touching hand to nose. "I'd better get going." He edged away into the bedroom and quickly climbed into his tuxedo. Before he left the room he looked around it, remembering the sight of Lynne stretched out on the bed, recalling the feel of her beneath him. He took one last deep breath of the perfume—of her, of them— that lingered in the air. No matter what happened now, he would always have that to remember.

Lynne was still sitting at the table when he came back into her study. He took her by the hand and led her over to the door. "I'll call you tomorrow," he said, hearing a certain hollowness in his voice.

"Take care of yourself, Josh." She pulled the collar of his jacket up over his neck. "It's cold out there. I just heard the weather report."

"Don't worry," he said. He pressed his lips to her forehead and walked out the door.

Lynne listened to his footsteps on the stairs and waited for the lobby door to click shut behind him before she closed the door to her apartment. Slowly she cleared up the breakfast dishes and went into the bedroom. She made up the bed, straightening the sheets reluctantly, as if by keeping them in their disheveled state she could somehow hold the night captive. But it was over and there might never be another like it. The night existed only in her memory and in Josh's memory, she reminded herself. She hadn't dreamed it or conjured it up. She had lived it with him, and nothing could change that, no matter what happened now.

As she moved away from the bed her bare foot brushed something soft. Looking down she saw the corsage. A brushfire flared in her as she remembered how Josh had trailed it across her body. She picked it up carefully and held it close to her cheek for a moment. The delicate scent had evaporated already.

Ever so slowly, Lynne walked into her study and placed the orchids between two of the pages in her thickest dictionary. The flowers would dry, become brittle and eventually crumble, but something—even if it was only the merest fragment—would remain of the night she had danced away and loved away with Josh.

7

JENNY HOWARD ROSE WEARILY from her desk, stretched her arms high over her head, and then bent over at the waist, letting her arms dangle in front of her, feeling the strained muscles in her back and neck begin to loosen. She'd been at her desk since after lunch—six solid hours—working on the first draft of her doctoral thesis. She stood upright and straightened her papers, knowing that she'd accomplished as much as she had the stamina for today.

A grumbling stomach led Jenny to the refrigerator. She cut a couple of slices off a wedge of cheddar and took a few crackers from the jar on the counter. Though she had planned to stay in for the evening, she was feeling a slight attack of cabin fever—she'd been at home almost the entire weekend working on her thesis. An evening out would be just the thing before starting to teach again in the morning.

Jenny stretched out on the couch and nibbled at her cheese and crackers, wishing she had made plans beforehand. In New York there was little casual dropping in on friends; dates had to be made days or weeks in advance. She made a mental survey of friends who might be available for a last-minute, Sunday-night dinner or movie, stopping at Lynne with a speculative, "Hmm."

Jenny reached behind her to the end table for the

phone and brought it around to rest on her tummy. Lynne had taken Josh to that dinner-dance last night, and Jenny was most anxious to hear about the evening. Maybe they could go down to Chinatown....

LYNNE PULLED ANOTHER CHUNK of manuscript pages out of the box on the floor beside her chair and tucked the afghan more tightly around her curled-up legs. It was getting on to seven o'clock and she had made little progress on the manuscript she was reading, or trying to read. She couldn't seem to keep her mind on it, or on anything—except Josh. After he'd left she'd gone out for a Sunday newspaper, but she'd rifled through it without retaining the sense of any of the articles she'd read. Even the crossword puzzle, which she attacked with vigor every Sunday, paled after she'd filled in the first corner. Vague mumbles from her stomach reminded her she'd eaten nothing but some toast all day. She was thinking halfheartedly of heating up some soup for supper when the phone rang.

Lynne pounced on the ringing receiver. "Hello?" The female voice that responded stilled her thumping heart. He wasn't going to call tonight.

"Hi! It's Jenny."

Lynne responded as brightly as she could.

Sensing some preoccupation on Lynne's part, Jenny asked, "I'm not interrupting anything, am I?" Could it be possible that Josh was still there? "You don't have company, do you?"

"No, no. I was in the middle of reading a manuscript. The phone startled me, that's all."

There was a short silence before Jenny realized

that Lynne wasn't going to say anything else. "You don't have to work tonight, do you? I was looking for someone to play with. I've been in working all weekend and I need a break."

"I'm sorry, but I have to finish this tonight," Lynne said. She hated telling lies, even little white ones like that, but Jenny was the last person in the world she wanted to see tonight—or any time soon. *What a mess this all is,* Lynne thought. *Jenny is head over heels for Josh, Josh is dating Jenny, and now Josh and I start an affair.* "Why don't I call you sometime and we can get together," Lynne said vaguely.

"Can't you knock off for an hour, Lynne? I can come uptown and we can have a quick meal somewhere near your apartment. I've hardly talked to anyone all weekend." Jenny began to wonder what was going on with Lynne. She'd never been that anxious to read a manuscript before.

"Sorry, Jenny, but I can't. Look, I'll call you next week." Lynne was just about to say goodbye when Jenny interrupted.

"Hey, don't hang up. I want to hear all about the dinner-dance. Just five minutes, Lynne. That manuscript won't run away."

Only by being utterly rude could Lynne hang up now. Briefly she described the ballroom, the meal, the band, the guests. "Lilian Mason even remembered me and called me by name," Lynne reported, hoping that with that intimate detail she could get off the phone. "And that's about—"

"Lilian Mason!" Jenny exclaimed, cutting her off. "Josh must have been in seventh heaven. He told me he's a great fan of hers. Did he get to meet her?"

"He even danced with her," Lynne said, feeling

jealous that she'd never heard about Josh's fancy for Lilian Mason before last night.

"Phew!" Jenny breathed. "Is he a good dancer?"

"Quite good," Lynne said, remembering the feel of his arms around her, the breathlessness that had only partly come from the physical exertion. She didn't want to talk to anyone about Josh, especially Jenny who had her own interest in him. *Why couldn't I just leave well enough alone*, Lynne asked herself peevishly. *But no, I had to go around being a matchmaker.*

"I knew it. He's too good to be true, Lynne. I can't understand why no one's snatched him up before this. But I have a feeling that someone will, before too long." Jenny smiled to herself. She wondered how long it was going to take those two to figure out that they were perfect for each other. "I guess you must be tired," Jenny went on mischievously. "Did you stay out late?"

"The band didn't stop playing until after three," Lynne answered evasively.

Jenny whistled softly. "You must have had a wonderful time."

Lynne heard envy not approval in Jenny's words, and didn't reply. "I'm afraid I really have to get back to work now, Jenny. I'll talk to you soon." She put the receiver down and uncurled her legs. Though she wasn't at all hungry, she went into the kitchen to heat some soup, knowing she wouldn't get any reading done tonight. She had to do something to pass the time.

Jenny hung up the phone and tapped a fingernail thoughtfully on the receiver. Lynne's evening with Josh had to have been a terrific success. Had it been a disaster she surely would have wanted to talk about it. It never occurred to Jenny that she was one of the reasons Lynne had been so reluctant to speak.

JOSH DIDN'T GET HOME from work until after nine o'clock on Monday evening. There'd been a long meeting with one of his firm's most important clients in the morning, and a report to finish for another meeting first thing Tuesday. If his concentration had been better he'd have been out of the office by seven. But his thoughts had marched off to Lynne all day like a persistent and endless army of ants in pursuit of a particularly delectable crumb. He'd had quite a time mustering the troops to attend to spread sheets and earnings projections.

He shucked his topcoat and suit jacket and slipped off his already loosened tie. In the kitchen he popped open a beer and fixed himself a sandwich. Since leaving Lynne's apartment the previous afternoon he'd been trying to assess his feelings, but they didn't line up in neat columns like the data he called up on his computer terminal. Certainly he'd never spent a night like that before. It wasn't only the sex—that had been spectacular—but the whole way it had happened, as if it was inevitable, though he had only once before been conscious of so much as wanting to kiss her. What didn't add up on the balance sheet was the way his previous relationship with Lynne seemed only marginally related to what had happened on Saturday night. And the extreme discomfort he'd felt the day after, as if he—they—had done something wrong, something they should be ashamed of. No matter how he juggled the figures he couldn't come up with the right totals.

Josh finished off his sandwich and popped open another beer. He had promised to call Lynne today and he'd put it off every time he thought about it—both by way of prolonging a pleasure and avoiding a potentially painful experience. What if she had decided they'd made a terrible mistake, that she didn't want to see him again? That notion, added to his own uncertainty, increased his nervousness about making the call. He downed half the beer for courage and dialed her number.

Lynne forced herself to wait until the phone had rung twice before she picked it up.

"Hi," Josh said. "I just got home," he explained hastily before she could reply.

"Oh. Everything okay at the office?" she asked, trying to hide the relief in her voice that sounded so clear to her ears. As the minutes had ticked by that night she'd told herself many times that he'd been delayed at work. That had been to stop her thinking about the other possibilities: he'd forgotten he'd promised to call her; he didn't want to talk to her at all.

"Fine. Just busy."

There was a short but too-long pause.

"How are you?"

"Okay. A little—" she hesitated for a second, then added "—tired."

"That's understandable. I'm a little—" he made the same hesitation "—tired myself."

There was a longer pause.

"It's good to hear your voice, Josh," Lynne blurted out.

"Yours, too."

There was an even longer pause that Josh broke by

suddenly bursting into laughter. "This is crazy," he said. "We sound like two tongue-tied teenagers."

"Two tired tongue-tied teenagers," Lynne added with a much-welcome chuckle.

Josh groaned loudly in response. After that, conversation was easier. They chatted about inconsequential things for a few minutes, bantering and joking with each other, until Josh found himself stifling a yawn in the middle of a sentence.

"I think I'd better get some sleep," he said. "But feel free to stay up late reading tonight. That way I'll be able to take advantage of you on the court tomorrow."

"But you've already taken advantage of me," Lynne said lightly. She had spoken before she realized the implications of her words.

"I hope you don't think that, Lynne," Josh responded icily.

"I didn't mean that the way it sounded. I mean, it came out the wrong way. I mean— Oh, Josh, I'm sorry." She wanted to reach across the telephone lines and touch him, stroke his face, make him realize that she had only uttered a very poor joke. But she also wondered how much of the truth had slipped out just then.

Josh thawed somewhat. "It's okay. I guess we're both a little sensitive right now," he told her.

"Only enough to feel each individual nerve ending," Lynne joked feebly.

"Yeah." Josh laughed mirthlessly. "Well, I'll see you in the morning."

"Good night, Josh. Sleep well," she said, biting off the endearment she would have added.

Despite his wishes that she do the same and the

pot of camomile tea she made herself, Lynne's reading light was on far into the night.

Josh listened to the radio for hours in the dark.

WHEN LYNNE ARRIVED at the squash club the next morning there was no sign of Josh. She sat on one of the carpeted banquettes outside the courts, watching a game through the glass door of the court next door to the one that had been assigned to her and Josh. Although the two players were evenly matched and playing a close game, Lynne looked up so many times to see if Josh was coming that she lost track of what was going on in the court. She finally grabbed her racket and a ball and went onto the court to warm up.

Josh stood outside the court for a moment when he arrived, watching Lynne smash what certainly would have been a winning shot off the left corner of the court. She looked strong, powerful, determined, and it was hard for Josh to believe she was the same pliant yielding woman he had held in his arms less than two days ago. But when he rapped on the door with his racket and she turned to him, he recognized the smile. The ball she had been about to hit skittered to the floor. He opened the door and walked onto the court.

"Hello," she said, not moving to meet him.

"Hello. I didn't think I was late...."

"You're not. I think I was early. But it doesn't matter."

She still stood her ground, and Josh moved toward her. Half of him wanted to run and kiss the stuffing out of her, but the squash court was so unromantic—white and stark, the shouts and grunts of the other players echoing through the cavernous rooms. So he put his hands on her shoulders and pecked her lightly on the check. For a brief second she seemed about to press against him, but she accepted his kiss as it was and stepped away.

"Do you want to warm up for a few minutes?" she asked.

"No, that's all right. Let's just play."

"Spin for serve?" She placed her racket on the floor, edge of the head down. "You call."

"Rough," Josh chose.

"Sorry," Lynne said, examining the racket when it had stopped spinning. "It's smooth."

Sorry, Josh thought. Last Friday she would have clapped her hands and made some challenging comment to him about her unbreakable service. Josh was about to make a crack, but Lynne was in position, waiting to play.

Josh took his position and easily returned the first serve, which had none of Lynne's usual unpredictable spin on it, with a hard forehand shot. She rushed to the back of the court to retrieve it and aimed her return straight for the corner. The ball had more force than Josh had calculated and he ran backward to make the shot while Lynne was coming forward in anticipation of the next ball. His forearm brushed against her breast as she passed him; her eyes shot open and she glanced at him. It was only a split-second hesitation, but it caused her to miss the shot and lose service.

Lynne chided herself under her breath as she waited for Josh to serve. They had made body contact countless times before on the court—it was inevitable while playing squash—but it had never

Just Friends   111

made her lose a point. Many more brushes like that and she'd lose the game, and she wouldn't want Josh to think for a second that she let him win just because they'd spent the night together.

It's a good thing she lost that point, Josh said to himself as he prepared to serve. *Because I'd surely have lost the next one.* A single brush with her body and he had developed a hyperawareness of what was beneath the brief shorts and T-shirt—her full breasts, the gently rounded stomach. He took a deep breath and smashed out the hardest serve he could.

They played silently and hard for the next several points, but for both it was like trying to play on the deck of a sailboat—against the sea swell of emotions balance was difficult to maintain. Lynne finally found a solid footing and made a brilliant shot. Josh was sure he wouldn't be able to reach it, but he lunged and somehow connected with the ball. No sooner had he seen that his shot was good than he called out, "Sorry." Sorry? For making one of the best shots he'd ever made? Josh didn't know whether to laugh or to hit himself over the head with his racket.

Lynne missed the return, and Josh waited to hear the usual barrage of salty words that she uttered in situations like these. But all he heard was a meek, "Your point." *She must really be upset,* Josh thought, and when she made her next tough shot he let it roll by him with only a pretense of an effort to get to it.

"What did you do that for?" Lynne asked sharply.

"Do what?"

"Deliberately miss that point."

"I tried to get it," Josh said unconvincingly.

"Josh, you don't have to treat me differently just because we—"

"I don't want to do that," he broke in. He wanted to please her, to make her happy, but he was unsure of how to do it now that everything felt so different, so out of kilter.

"Then don't," she said flatly. They'd stood here on this court so many times before, but this morning, though they were playing the same game, it seemed that all the rules had been changed.

They continued the game with scrupulous care and politeness, and when the bell rang Lynne was up by one point—the point Josh had let her have before and had never struggled to regain. She didn't feel like she'd achieved a victory. In fact, it seemed like they'd both lost—and more than just a squash game.

"Nice game," Josh remarked listlessly as they left the court. He didn't know why he hadn't fought harder to regain that point he'd given up. But he felt constrained with Lynne today, wary, as if he had to hold back the full force of his feelings.

"Meet you in the lobby," Lynne said, picking up her gear and smiling grimly. "Unless you'd rather skip breakfast."

"No, no, I'm looking forward to it," Josh said.

For a moment they devoured each other with eyes rife with longing and questions. Each seemed about to say something, but both turned wordlessly and went their separate ways.

"JUST SOME WHOLE-WHEAT TOAST and coffee," Lynne told the waiter at the Apollo. Josh looked at her with a raised eyebrow. "Not hungry," she said.

"The usual for me, Tony," Josh said to the waiter. "Are you all right, Lynne?"

"Why shouldn't I be?" She apologized immediately for her harsh tone. "A little edgy about work, I guess." The answer was truthful enough, though hardly complete. Her first day at work with the new editor in chief, who had been brought into Parker and Hamilton from another firm, had not been one to inspire feelings of warmth and confidence in an easy working relationship. "I'm so used to having Alan there as a mentor, I'm feeling a bit exposed. Friendless, you could say." The new man had subjected several of her projects to close and critical scrutiny. "We've all been promised, of course, that there will be no major staff changes, but one way or another heads always roll when there's a new boss."

While Josh downed his eggs and bacon and Lynne nibbled at her toast, they talked about the situation at her office, about Josh's work, about current events, even the weather—everything but what had happened between them. When each had finished another cup of coffee, Lynne began to gather her briefcase and purse.

"I'd better be going, Josh. I have a lot of work to get through today."

Josh was about to rise but thought better of it. "Stay for two more minutes, Lynne." He reached across the table for her hand, grazing her fingertips with his. "We can't go on pretending nothing happened Saturday night."

Lynne closed her eyes briefly and then looked down at the table, anywhere but at Josh. She was sure he was going to say it had all been a mistake, that they had gotten carried away. "No, we can't," she agreed softly.

"I'm not sorry," Josh said. "A little off-balance,

maybe, as if I'm walking around on one of those teeterboards they use in the circus." He made a swaying motion with his hand that Lynne saw out of the corner of her eye. "But definitely not sorry."

The weight that had been pressing ever more heavily on Lynne for the past two days lightened somewhat. She looked up at him. "Me, either, Josh. It's just that—"

"I know. What happens next? Why don't we take it one step at a time, Lynnie? Build on what we've got, try to find a new balance." He pressed her hand tightly. "It's going to take time to get to know each other in a new way."

Lynne squeezed his hand in return. "When can we get started?"

"Not as soon as I'd like," Josh said ruefully, running a single finger up and down her forearm. "I'm off to Chicago early tomorrow morning and won't be back until Friday afternoon. But we can spend Friday evening together and take it from there." He made a motion with his hand like a jet plane taking off and accompanied it with a soft whoosh.

"Where do you think we're headed, Josh?"

His face grew serious and his eyes darkened. He had as few answers to the question as she did. "As far as we can go," he said quietly. "As far as we *want* to go."

8

LYNNE'S EYES ADJUSTED SLOWLY to the dim light in the Second Avenue bar where Josh had suggested they meet. As she'd expected, the place was lined two- and three-deep with hardworking young professionals easing themselves from the care-filled week into the carefree weekend. When Josh had called from the airport, she'd thought of offering an alternate, more-quiet meeting place, but the call was interrupted by the recorded voice that anounced the end of the initial time limit, so she said yes quickly before they were cut off.

She tried to pick Josh from among the suited Wall Street types but only spotted him when someone moved and she caught a flash of something long and white and flowing. He was standing at the end of the bar in jeans and his leather jacket, a white silk aviator's scarf thrown around his neck. Though the anxiety she'd been feeling all day about seeing him did not entirely disappear, her heart made a small joyous skip at the sight of him.

Josh adjusted his stance every time the crowd shifted, craning his neck to keep an eye on the door, watching for Lynne. But the entrance was hard to keep in sight. It went out of view for a minute or so. When he was able to see it again he spotted her standing there, looking slightly lost or perhaps perplexed—it was hard to read facial expressions at a distance in this light—but as clean and forthright as always. He liked that so much about her. There were no layers of pretense in her, no wish to obscure or hide her feelings and opinions. He raised his hand high over his head and waved to her.

Lynne waved back to show she had seen him. After pushing her way through the crowd she wedged herself into a small space beside him. He tried to manage a welcoming embrace, but it was both awkward and conspicuous, so he leaned over and touched his lips to her cheek. It was still cold from the air outside.

"The last time I was in here—about six months ago—it was quiet and practically empty. It seems to have been discovered in the meantime. Would you like to go somewhere else?" Josh had to shout to be heard over the crowd and the rock music, even though Lynne's ear was only inches from his mouth.

Lynne pointed to the nearly full glass of beer in front of him. "You might as well finish your beer," she said.

"Would you like a drink?"

"When in Rome," she answered with a shrug.

It took a few minutes for Josh to catch the bartender's eye and another few minutes for the bartender to return with a glass of red wine for Lynne.

"How was Chicago?" she asked. With raucous laughter and conversation all around them it was impossible to ask or say anything more intimate.

"Cold and windy—and busy. I had meetings lined up from breakfast through dinner. But let's forget about that." He pointed his chin in the direction of their fellow patrons. "When in Rome..." he echoed her words with an ironic smile.

Lynne picked up her wineglass. Josh grabbed his glass and clinked it to hers. "To another evening full of surprises," he toasted, looking her full in the eyes.

Lynne felt flushed even before the wine had started a trail of warmth that ran from her lips over her tongue and down her throat to her stomach. For a moment the crowd seemed to disappear, the loud conversation and music to die off. But then she realized that Josh was trying to say something else to her. She could see his mouth moving, but she couldn't hear a word.

"What did you say?" she shouted over the din.

"I said, what shall we do tonight? Unless you'd like to stay here," he said with a grin.

"Thanks, I'll pass. Otherwise, I don't care, as long as its quiet."

"What?"

"Quiet!" she yelled.

"I didn't say a word." They both laughed and Josh picked up his glass and drained it. He motioned to her to do the same. Lynne took a few fast sips until the glass was half-empty, and then tugged at his scarf.

They picked their way through the crowd to the door.

"Sorry about that," Josh said when they were out on the street. After the bar, Second Avenue, with its traffic and honking taxis, seemed as quiet as a church.

"I should have said something when you called this afternoon. I knew it was going to be like that."

"Why didn't you?"

"I don't know. I didn't want us to get cut off, and I didn't want you to think—" She stopped short. Why was she trying so hard with him?

Josh draped an arm around her shoulder. "We've got to be honest with each other, Lynne. We've never pandered to each other's egos before. There's no reason to start now."

"I know. It was silly." They walked to the corner and stopped at the light. "Shall we decide where we're going, so we'll know which way to cross?"

"I could use something to eat," Josh said. "And maybe we could see a movie afterward," he added tentatively. "I'm sorry I've been out of town. I would have planned something special."

"Now don't you start apologizing," Lynne admonished. "I was here. I could have made some plans."

"There was no reason for you to do that."

The light had changed twice and they were still standing on the same corner. Lynne, mimicking the gesture Josh had made in the Apollo on Tuesday morning, slapped her palms together and shot one of her hands skyward. "Let's just see where it takes us," she said teasingly. They both laughed and Josh grabbed her hand and pulled her across Second Avenue.

"Food?" he asked.

"Yes, please."

"Where?"

Lynne closed her eyes and turned around in a circle. When she stopped and opened her eyes she was facing downtown. She pointed down the avenue.

They walked for a couple of blocks and Josh

stopped in front of a Japanese restaurant he'd never noticed before. It was new and sleek with black-tinted windows. Behind the center window a stark arrangement of reeds and bare branches in a black-and-white vase was lit by a single spotlight. Josh took a long look at the vase and then at the menu displayed discreetly in the corner of the window. "I've never eaten here," he said. "Do you like Japanese food?"

The front of the restaurant said to Lynne that the owners had a high regard for style and atmosphere, something that rarely correlated with casual dining. But the place had attracted Josh for some reason. "Do you?" she asked, wondering if he had a special interest in Japanese food.

"I asked first."

"I like it," Lynne answered. It wasn't her favorite cuisine, but she could enjoy it once in a while—as long as it wasn't raw fish.

Although the distinctive design of the restaurant had caught his attention as they passed, after looking it over Josh decided that the place looked too highly stylized for his taste. But from her answer to his question he wasn't sure what Lynne thought. She hadn't sounded especially eager, but she had looked closely at the restaurant window, and had seemed to be intrigued with the place. "Shall we give it a try?" he asked.

"Sure," Lynne said, mustering some enthusiasm.

They were shown to a square black table by a young Japanese woman with a short severe haircut wearing a billowing black dress that looked to Lynne like a kimono designed by a parachute maker. The table was not the average American height, nor was it the low Japanese table; it was somewhere in between. The angular black lacquer chairs looked like their legs had been sawed off. Lynne wanted desperately to laugh at the trendiness and pretension of the place, but for Josh's sake kept her face poker straight and added a veneer of polite interest.

This place must have been designed by an angry short person, Josh said to himself as he lowered his limbs carefully into the chair. He was about to voice his thoughts, but a glance at Lynne's serious expression changed his mind. It wasn't the sort of place he would have expected her to like, but she was looking at the room with interest, or so it seemed to him.

Josh ordered sake when the menus were brought, and they sipped the warm potent wine as they made their choices. Though the place was nearly empty it took quite a while for the food to arrive, during which time they made desultory conversation. Lynne began to experience a strange sensation—as if she and Josh were on different icebergs drifting farther and farther apart in cold ocean currents. She wanted to wave to him to come back, or paddle her iceberg in the same direction as his, but was afraid to, afraid that he might take off even faster in the opposite direction.

When their food came Lynne couldn't understand what had taken so long to prepare. In the middle of her plate—unrelievedly black again—there were four thin slices of chicken artfully arranged among four tiny long-stemmed mushrooms and four strands of what looked like seaweed. She wasn't sure if she was supposed to eat the food or take a picture of the dish.

Josh looked at his plate with dismay—a few minute strips of beef surrounded by some strange-looking vegetables. He was very hungry, but what he had been served wouldn't feed a midget who'd been on a food binge all day. Remembering some advice to dieters he'd once read in a magazine, he ate very slowly, chewing each bite carefully and putting down his chopsticks every so often.

Neither Lynne nor Josh said anything about the food or about much else as they ate, or afterward as they sipped the green tea that was served at the meal's conclusion. Though a few more tables had been filled since they came into the restaurant, the diners talked only in sporadic whispers.

Josh tried to figure out what it was about the place that discouraged conversation. It was as if everyone was afraid to disturb the atmosphere, as if talking—or eating for that matter—had been deemed too crudely human for the rarified minimal design. Damned strange activities to suppress in a restaurant, he thought sourly. But he had only himself to blame, he knew. It was he who had suggested they eat here. He wondered what Lynne was thinking, but her face was set in a benign but distant semi-smile—rather like the Mona Lisa's—that said her thoughts were her own.

Lynne looked down into her pale green tea. *If this had happened a couple of weeks ago,* she thought glumly, *we'd both be laughing our heads off about the whole ridiculous situation. And after this place we'd stop at the nearest pizza stand for a slice or two. What's wrong with Josh? Or with me, for that matter?* The answer seemed to waft from the steam in the tea. One little three letter word: sex. Nothing like it to put kinks in even the most-comfortable relationships. She and

Josh used to be like a pair of well-worn sneakers; now they were more like a pair of stiff new high heels that pinched and rubbed.

Outside the restaurant the color and liveliness of Second Avenue felt as refreshing as a cold shower on a muggy August day. Lynne took a grateful gulp of the thick air and blinked her eyes against the bright but welcome streetlights. They walked down Second Avenue.

"Still feel like seeing a movie?" Josh asked. "Are there any comedies we can catch nearby?" What this evening needed was a few laughs to clear the increasingly heavy air. "Anything, that is, that won't have a line from here to Chicago. I just came from there this morning and I'm not all that eager to go back soon." He smiled hopefully, like a not-too-confident comedian begging his audience to like him. Lynne manufactured a laugh in response, but it sounded as false as it was.

"I'm not sure, but I can look. I came prepared," Lynne said brightly, pulling the movie pages from the morning paper out of her purse.

"Good Girl Scouts never die," Josh mumbled as they stopped in front of a delicatessen to read through the listings in the light coming from its window.

Lynne chose to ignore what seemed to her a very sarcastic remark.

"How about the new Woody Allen movie?" Josh suggested, pointing to the ad for it in the paper.

"It just opened this week, Josh. Forget Chicago. The line will be all the way to California," Lynne said.

They considered two or three other movies with a

degree of mutual interest, but found that they had just missed the beginning of the shows and the next showings didn't begin for anywhere from an hour and a half to two hours. Lynne started scanning the ads looking at show times. The only movie they could get to in time for the start was a French film playing on Third Avenue, just a few blocks downtown from where they were standing.

"Do you know anything about it?" Josh asked.

"Not really," she replied, although she'd skimmed an unfavorable review in *New York* magazine. But it had been written by a critic with whose judgment she didn't often agree, so she decided not to bring it up. Maybe it would turn out to be good. If nothing else it might untie their tongues. "We'll just make it if we hurry," she said, stuffing the newspaper pages back into her purse.

They walked briskly over to Third Avenue and down to the theater. As they passed through the lobby the smell of fresh hot popcorn drew Josh like a magnet, but stoically he walked past the refreshment stand. The lights had already dimmed when they entered the long narrow auditorium. It was quite full and the only two seats together were in the second row. The screen was set high in the front wall so they had to crane their necks to see it.

As the opening credits began to roll, Lynne slumped down in her seat, trying to find a better angle at which to view the screen. The handsome, dark-haired man descending into the Paris Metro looked as if he was tilted backward, but no matter how she twisted, she couldn't find a position in which the action on the screen would appear upright. Her eyes tired quickly of reading the subtitles at that angle, and after a while she stopped trying and let the words bounce off her ears, catching as much of the dialogue as her rusty college French would allow.

The action—what little there was of it—wasn't hard to follow. A professor obsessed with one of his students followed her surreptitiously and was alternately aroused and angered by her activities. The film was shot in a flat realistic style and moved at a relentlessly slow pace. Lynne's attention wandered hither and thither, but never strayed far from an awareness of Josh's restless movements in the chair next to hers.

As an adult, Josh had never been embarrassed by erotic scenes in the cinema, but when the professor finally gained the object of his desire—although it was impossible to say whether or not the event took place only in the professor's imagination—Josh found himself growing as hot and red faced as a twelve-year-old. But even at twelve he'd have had less qualms about reaching over and holding his date's hand during the kissing scenes than he was having now as a grown man thinking about taking Lynne's hand in his. He wanted to, but an impenetrable barrier seemed to be erecting itself between them. He had no idea where it had come from. He hadn't willed it to appear—and he didn't think Lynne had, either—but there it was, like a rude and unwanted guest spoiling what had started out to be a lovely party.

The love scene being played on the screen was not graphic or explicit or distasteful, but even had it been, Lynne could hardly have been more unwilling to watch it. As every minute of this evening with

Josh had ticked away the love scene they had played the week before seemed to become more and more remote. Instead of bringing it closer, the action on the screen made it even more distant—the way films seen in the past become more dimly remembered with every succeeding film you see, each scene displaced by fresher newer ones. If only Josh would reach for her hand she might be able to get a clear print of the scene the two of them had played so beautifully. She felt him stir and she put her arm on the rest between their seats, but he shifted his weight farther from her. Lynne let her hand drop back into her lap.

The movie ended as it had begun, with the dark-haired handsome professor in the Metro, except now he was ascending the stairs. Perhaps that was the point of the movie, Lynne thought, stretching her legs in front of her. The director was trying to indicate how much of our lives are lived "underground"—in our minds. As they waited for the crowd to file out of the theater she asked Josh, "Did that last shot mean that the whole thing took place in the professor's mind, that it was just a fantasy he had while riding the train?"

"Could be," Josh answered. "Films like this leave a lot to the imagination." *And a lot to be desired,* he added silently.

Lynne tried to draw Josh into a discussion of the film as they walked back up Third Avenue toward her apartment. But his answers were perfunctory at first and then monosyllabic. She lapsed into a silence that Josh didn't break. They hadn't said anything to each other for blocks when they reached Lynne's building.

"Would you like to come up for coffee?" she asked, not wanting the evening to end before it had started. She wanted to understand how in the space of a few short hours they had come to walk parallel, rather than intersecting, lines.

Josh didn't know what to say. The look on her face mirrored his own interior confusion. He reached out and stroked her cheek, which was soft but also cold from their walk in the brisk fall night air. *All we need is to touch a little bit,* he thought to himself. He cupped her other cheek and drew her face close to his. "I could use something warm."

Lynne closed her eyes briefly, her face suddenly flushed from his touch. She leaned forward, then rested her head against his shoulder, expecting his arms to surround her, but they didn't. Disappointed, she pushed away from him and rifled in her bag for her keys.

Josh followed her up the stairs and into the apartment. "I'll make the coffee. Why don't you have a seat in the living room?" The words came out taut and strained and masked the questions she really wanted to ask. *What's going on here? Why is this happening?*

"Can I help?" Josh asked.

"I think I can manage to make a pot of coffee by myself, Josh." She dropped her jacket on her reading chair and went into the kitchen.

Feeling helpless—he had little experience in situations where he felt out of control—Josh wandered into the living room. Because of the setup of Lynne's railroad flat, he had to pass through the bedroom first. He stopped in front of the bed, unable to walk by without remembering the feel of her in his arms.

If only they could go back in time and live that night over and over again. He would never tire of that. But the door to that magic place seemed to have been bolted behind them. And he wasn't sure what had happened to the key.

Lynne busied herself in the kitchen grinding coffee beans and pouring milk into a small pitcher while waiting for the water to boil. She tried to get herself to simmer down. The more she thought of it the more she was sure that look in his eyes when he'd touched her cheek outside had been one of someone who had bad news to deliver. He was going to tell her he thought they'd made a mistake, that they should go back to being just friends. That's why he'd asked her out tonight. To say goodbye, not hello.

The sharp whistle of the kettle pierced the quiet. She turned the gas off and the whistle died to a moan, then a hiss. It was her own fault, she said to herself, for expecting tonight to be a continuation of last Saturday. The last drops of coffee splashed into the pot, and Lynne tossed the filter and grinds into the trash can as if tossing aside dreams that had been leached of all their flavor.

When she entered the living room Josh was sitting on the couch, leaning forward, elbows resting on knees, the picture of a man lost in thought. He straightened when he saw her and moved from the center of the sofa to the end nearest the windows. Lynne put the tray down and poured the coffee. Without asking or thinking she put cream and sugar in his and handed him the mug.

Josh took a sip. "Just right," he said.

Lynne sat down beside him and sipped her coffee

without really tasting it. She was aware of a sensation of heat as it flowed down her throat, but of little else. She felt like a prisoner awaiting sentencing. How would he start? *I've been thinking, Lynne....* *About last Saturday, Lynne....* But instead of hearing words she felt the mug being gently pried from her hand, and Josh's arm circling her shoulders. With his other arm he pressed her against the back of the couch. His mouth touched hers. She held her breath and didn't move, waiting for the kiss to deepen.

The minute I touched her she went stiff as a board, Josh thought with dismay. He moved away from her and retreated to his own corner of the couch. "Sorry," he mumbled.

Lynne sat up and looked away from him. "I guess this isn't going to work, is it, Josh?" she asked in a small voice. It was easier to say it herself than to hear it from him. Somehow it hurt less. "This hasn't been a great evening—for either of us." When he didn't answer she added uncertainly, "Has it?"

"No, I guess not."

"Just one of those things," she said lamely.

He took her hand lightly in his. "I don't know what happened."

"Me, either."

"Lynnie, Lynnie," he whispered.

The room was so quiet Lynne thought she could hear the steam spiraling up from the coffeepot, vanishing into the cold still air. Long weighty seconds passed, and when she could no longer bear it she stole a glance at Josh.

Josh felt the furtive movement of her eyes and turned toward her. Their eyes met, overflowing with feeling. Instinctively he reached for her. His arms closed around her and he drew her to him. When he kissed her he felt no resistance and so increased the pressure on her mouth. She did not move away, but neither did she yield to him. Suddenly Josh wanted to overpower her, to show her how much he wanted her despite her reserve, her fears. He ran his hands roughly up and down her back and snaked his tongue between her closed teeth.

Lynne pushed away from his harsh lips with a desperate cry. She didn't want him to make love to her just because he thought she wanted him to, to show her that he could, that he was capable of pleasing her even when his heart wasn't in it. "This isn't right, Josh," she said, straightening herself and moving away from him.

"No," he agreed, ashamed at how easily the urge to use force had come to him. "I shouldn't have done that."

"We need to talk, Josh," Lynne said after several silent moments.

"I'm sorry about tonight—"

"Let's not start apologizing," Lynne said, interrupting him. "No one is to blame for anything that happened. If we're going to start that we might as well say it's my fault for inviting you to Alan's retirement dinner." She plunged ahead. "I'm not sorry about what happened last Saturday, but there's no sense in trying to go any further if...if both of us don't want to." Now that she had started talking she felt like a windup doll whose key had been wound too tightly. She had to keep going. "Neither of us signed any contracts, made any promises. We were thrown into a very romantic situation, we had too much champagne and danced too closely, and...

well...one thing led to another. It was lovely, but there's no obligation for either of us to try to recreate any feelings we—" Lynne stopped, exhausted, as if she had used up all her breath.

"Does that mean you don't want to see me at all anymore?" Josh asked quietly. After all she had said he had nothing to add. She'd spoken so strongly that there didn't seem to be anything he could say that would change her mind.

"Not want to see you!" Lynne heard the panic she was feeling in her high-pitched words. She managed a laugh to cover it. "You're my friend, Josh," she said more evenly.

"So you just want to go back to square one, forget we ever...we ever went to bed together. Forget that we ever made love," he added baldly.

"I don't want to forget it." Even if she wanted to she couldn't forget it, Lynne thought.

"But it would be better if we didn't continue in that direction," he said with a touch of sarcasm.

"That's one way of putting it." *If that's the way you want it*, she said sadly to herself.

Her words sounded final and irrevocable to Josh. He stood up and took his jacket and scarf from the arm of the couch. "I guess I'll see you around the squash club sometime."

"Sometime? What about Tuesday morning?" Lynne rose and forced herself not to put a restraining hand on his arm.

"Do you still want to play?"

"Of course. I don't want to lose a squash partner." She assumed a bantering tone. "Not after I've spent all this time getting you up to my standard." But the words sounded crass, with an arrogant, almost-cruel edge.

Just Friends 131

"And I wouldn't want to miss the chance to show you what a good teacher you've been," he said with an oblique and cutting smile. Torn between kissing some sense into her and shaking the nonsense out of her, he shrugged into his jacket and turned to go. "Good night, Lynne."

"I'll show you to the door," she said, following him to the archway that led to the bedroom. But on the threshold she stopped. She couldn't bear to walk through the bedroom with him.

Josh glanced into the room and back at Lynne. "That won't be necessary," he replied. The words actually hurt his throat, but he hoped the pain didn't show. He stalked out of the apartment.

Lynne heard the door slam and rushed through the bedroom into the study. She had her hand on the door and was about to fling it open and call him back when she heard the lobby door shut with a final bang. She collapsed in her reading chair and sat there numbly for an indeterminate amount of time. It might have been five minutes or an hour. Inside she felt hollow, empty of all feelings. She knew she should feel hurt, angry, tired, upset, bereft, but she didn't. Or couldn't allow herself to.

Her stomach began to contract and whine. She put a staying hand on it, but the grumbles just grew louder. *My lover, my friend has just walked out my door, and all I can feel is hungry,* she chided herself. In the kitchen she slapped some peanut butter and jam on a piece of bread and downed it with a glass of milk. Her stomach stopped growling, but her hunger was unappeased.

JOSH STRODE DETERMINEDLY down the street toward his apartment, but an hour later he was still wandering the streets of the upper East Side. The night had turned cold, his leather jacket was inadequate protection, and his stomach was yelling loudly for something to eat. He stopped in an all-night coffee shop and ordered a rare hamburger and a cup of coffee. The cup warmed his hands and the liquid took the chill from his insides. When his hamburger was served he ate it quickly. Still hungry, he ordered another, but after taking a single bite of it he realized that this lingering hunger had nothing to do with a lack of food. He left the hardly touched burger on the plate and walked home.

9

LYNNE STOOD OUTSIDE the squash court for several minutes, watching Josh bash the ball against the front wall with hard determined strokes. He returned the hard-hit balls in a sure even rhythm, until one bounced on a higher trajectory than he had anticipated. He was not quick enough to adjust and missed the shot. That was the weakness in his game, the reason she could beat him despite his superior physical strength. She was faster, more agile and could change direction easier to accommodate the unexpected. Still, the rigid set of Josh's mouth told her he would be a tough opponent this morning.

Last night she had thought of calling him to cancel the game, but now she was glad she hadn't. The sharp metallic taste in her mouth told her how very much she wanted to win this morning. Even though it couldn't make up for the losses she had incurred on Friday night, it would make a mark in the right column. She clenched her hand into a tight fist and knocked sharply on the door of the court.

At the sound of the raps, Josh reached up to stop the ball that was hurtling toward him. He scooped up the ball in his free hand and squeezed it. It was warm and alive from the half hour warm-up he'd just had. There would be no waiting for the ball to be ready for play this morning. He was glad he'd called the club yesterday and reserved the court for an extra half hour. Not only was the ball ready for play, he was, too. His muscles felt elastic and responsive, the racket like a natural extension of his arm, and his mind was in tune with the rhythm of play. It would take Lynne some time to catch up with him. He'd never cared so much about winning as he did this morning. Usually playing the game was more important, but this morning the need to win was a hunger that demanded satisfaction.

When the ball was out of play Lynne flung the door of the court open. "Hi," she said curtly.

"Hi," Josh answered, as if returning a hard serve.

"I'll take a few minutes to warm up," she announced.

Josh moved from center court to a rear corner and leaned against the wall. His heart was still pumping fast from the exertion, but the beat was steady, strong. He didn't feel the least bit tired. On the contrary, his energy reserves had been increased not depleted by the half hour's exercise. Lynne was warming up slowly, methodically increasing the force of her strokes. Josh sized her up as objectively as he would look at a spread sheet or a piece of financial data. To the feelings that inevitably arose— twinges of desire, sparks of anger, scratches of hurt—he ordered an about-face, turning them into foot soldiers he could call on in the upcoming battle.

With each stroke Lynne narrowed the focus of her attention until she reacted like a machine whose only function was to hit a ball with a racket. The process was like that of an orchestra tuning up; the individual instruments tootled, played scales and runs, but on the signal of the conductor came together to sound one perfect A. Lynne's muscles stretched and flexed. Her eyes became accustomed to picking out the black ball in the white room, and her mind was drained of all thoughts except putting racket to ball. She was aware of Josh watching her in the corner, but she pushed the awareness aside as a musician forgets about the microphone that will record a performance. It was there, but it couldn't be allowed to affect the playing of the piece.

When her body was ready and her concentration honed, Lynne let the ball drop out of play. She turned to Josh. "Spin for serve," she said quietly.

Josh won the spin and they took their positions on the court. With steely, unblinking eyes they regarded each other for a long moment of cool appraisal and heated challenge. Then Josh raised his racket and delivered a deadly serve.

The ball hit the wall with a forceful crack, and Lynne tensed her muscles to withstand the impact when the rebounding ball connected with her racket. She anticipated exactly where the ball would hit and with perfect timing stroked back a hard forehand shot calculated to put the ball over Josh's head. The ball went exactly where she had intended it to go, but Josh moved back swiftly and caught it, sending it caroming off the corner. Lynne dashed to the opposite corner and sent an easy shot straight ahead of her, thinking Josh would never reach the forecourt in time to get it. But he surprised her and hit a winning shot to the far backcourt out of Lynne's grasp.

Josh won three points before Lynne broke his service, giving him an enormous psychological advantage. On her serve she managed to win two points, but then missed on the third volley. Each point had become longer than the last, both players scrambling for—and reaching—balls they would not have attempted in other, more-friendly games. They were both breathing hard, drawing deep for the oxygen that powered their muscles.

Lynne managed to win back the service on the next point, keeping the score at 3–2 and dulling somewhat the edge Josh had established at the beginning of the game. She tied the score but was prevented from getting ahead by a crosscourt winner that sailed past her like a bird on the breeze. He had never played so well. The sudden, unexpected and now-unwelcome improvement in his game annoyed Lynne and made her even more determined to show him why she had been a nationally ranked competitor in college.

On an unusually long point, Lynne finally broke Josh's serve with a strategically placed corner carom that dribbled onto the forecourt, far from the reach of his racket. The excellent shot was psychologically damaging to Josh—losing a point after such a long volley was always hard on the loser—but the point had taken its toll on Lynne, too. She was gasping hard for breath, and she'd wrenched her wrist setting up the final shot.

The play continued and became harder and rougher for both players as they set up obstacles for each other and then knocked them over. The serve changed hands every point or two, neither of them establishing more than a one-point lead at any time. The score was tied when the bell rang. Court etiquette allowed them to play out a single tie-breaking point.

Josh had the advantage of the serve and slugged

out a shot that nearly whizzed right past Lynne. Only by executing a deep lunge did she reach the ball and scoop it up for the return. But the shot was weak and Josh easily caught it and sent the ball smashing onto the front wall. Like a cannonball it flew over Lynne's head. She jumped for it. Catching it by sheer luck, she tapped it lightly, hoping to make Josh miss the ball by having to run for it. But he anticipated her move and connected the exact center of his racket to the ball.

In this excellent play, not in a mistake, Lynne found her opening. She saw on Josh's face that he thought he had won, that he was sure she couldn't get to the ball this time. She saw him relax ever so slightly, thinking he would not have to return a shot. Imagining the exact spot behind her on the court where she could reach the ball, she started running backward without looking behind her, and keeping her eye fixed on the trajectory of the ball, calculated the swing she would make. She felt the ball connect with her racket and smashed it with shattering force to the opposite corner.

A second too late Josh jumped to get the rebound. The ball skimmed the top of his racket and skipped to the ground. It bounced a few times and rolled into a corner, leaving the court silent except for the sound of gasping breaths.

There was a rap on the Plexiglas back wall of the court. The next players gestured for permission to enter. Lynne waved them in and picked up the ball from the corner. She tossed it easily to Josh. "Yours, I think," she said between heavy breaths, and preceded him out of the court. She collapsed on the lowest carpeted tier and pulled a towel from her gym bag.

Josh seized a towel from his bag and mopped his dripping face. He draped it around his neck and picked up his bag. "At least it was an honest game today." He shot the words at her with the force of a speeding squash ball.

Surprised and stung, Lynne looked up at him. "What's that supposed to mean?"

"You won because you played a better game, not because I let you win, like last time." He started off in the direction of the men's locker room.

Lynne jumped up. "Don't walk away from me, Josh. I didn't ask you to let me win," she reproached. "In fact—"

"Spare me the accusations, Lynne," Josh interrupted. "The only thing I was guilty of then was harboring a few tender feelings for you. But don't worry, they're gone now."

Lynne felt like she'd been hit in the stomach with a medicine ball. A bitter medicine ball. "If I'd known that losing a squash game was going to make you feel like this, I'd have cancelled. You never seemed to mind losing to me before."

"Before what?"

Before today, Lynne was about to say, but that was not the truth. In a low voice she spoke the harsh words, "Before you slept with me."

Josh wanted to shout at her, but if they raised their voices they'd have an audience, so he struggled to keep an even tone. "You were there, too, in case you've forgotten."

"You're the one who seems to have forgotten," Lynne said, biting back the tears that were beginning to muddy her eyes.

"Me?" Josh asked with a hollow laugh.

"Ever since it happened you've been trying to act as if it hadn't, as if it was just another squash game... but with slightly different rules. We might play another casual game if we feel like it, but then again, we might not, which is the option you'd obviously prefer."

"Or the option you'd prefer, if you were being honest."

As if a referee had called a time-out, a silence lapsed between them, broken only by the muffled pings and twangs coming from the occupied courts. Lynne twisted her towel into a taut spiral; Josh removed the terry-cloth sweatband from his forehead and twirled it around his finger in a fitful circle. There was more to be said, but the words hovered around them like players on the sidelines waiting for the game to resume. Josh heard the whistle first.

"I think you're afraid." He tossed out the words to her. "What happened between us scared you, and you've been pushing me away ever since."

"At least I had some feelings about it," Lynne countered, returning the ball with a hard pass.

"And I didn't?"

"None visible to the naked eye."

"What did you expect me to do, Lynne? Fall all over you, profess undying love and devotion after one night in the sack?" The words were like a game-losing shot that Josh wished he could retract or play over. In an attempt to rectify his mistake he compounded the error. "I wouldn't have done that, even if I had been able to catch up with you. But you were running so hard in the opposite direction you lost me."

"I wasn't running anywhere, although it may

have seemed that way to someone who can only crawl. If you didn't want to see me anymore why didn't you just come right out and tell me instead of behaving like a slug?"

Josh clenched his anger tight between his teeth. "I thought I knew you pretty well, Lynne. But I was wrong. I thought you were tough-minded but fair, but now I see that you're pigheaded and narrow-minded. Jenny warned me you had a stubborn streak, and I was stupid enough to argue with her. I won't make that mistake again."

"Jenny?" Lynne said limply. "When did you see Jenny?"

"On Saturday night—not that it's any of your affair."

"No," Lynne replied, swallowing the sobs that threatened to overwhelm her, "it would appear to be yours and Jenny's." A single tear escaped from her right eye and she brushed it away savagely.

Josh shook his head sadly. "Whatever I say, you're going to believe what you want to believe." He turned his back on her and walked away.

Lynne watched him go, wanting to pursue him but unable to get the command to move from her brain to her feet. "Josh!" She called his name so loudly that the two players on the court glared at her. Under their angry eyes her feet moved automatically. "Stop," she said, putting a restraining hand on his arm. He shook her away but stopped walking.

"I think we've said everything we have to say to each other, Lynne," he said coldly.

"Why is this happening?" she asked plaintively.

"Because I'm an aloof bastard," he answered sarcastically. "And," he added cruelly, refusing to bend under the expression of terrible sorrow in her eyes, "you're a scared little girl, afraid to grow up, afraid to have a relationship that isn't black or white, yes or no." He turned away, sure that the look in his eyes, behind the thin blustering veneer, was no less sorrowful than the one in hers.

"I thought I knew you, too," Lynne whispered, barely able to force the words past her lips. "But I look at you now, and all I see is a stranger."

They stared at each other for several time-suspended seconds, each waiting for the other to reach out, to apologize, but they both stood firm in the rock-hard places they had carved for themselves.

Slowly Lynne came to the realization that it was over, not only the horrible fight, but everything. She and Josh were finished. She couldn't bear to look at him. "It appears we've proven the old cliché," she said, pain and weariness evident in her voice. "We should have left well enough alone."

Josh lifted his tired eyes for one last look at her. Her hair was disheveled, her T-shirt rumpled, but even through the veil of his hurt and anger she still looked beautiful to him. "I thought what we had, Lynne, was a damn sight better than 'well enough.'"

He left so quietly she was surprised to glance up and find him gone.

Numbly, Lynne picked up her gym bag and walked slowly to the women's locker room. With stiff ungainly hands she peeled off her shorts and T-shirt, wrapped a towel around her and headed for the showers. Until the steaming spray hit the top of her head she felt incapable of any but the most mechanical movements. But when the hot water poured over her, plastering her hair to her scalp, wetting her cold clammy skin, it released a torrent of terrible silent sobs. She crossed her arms over her stomach, as if to keep herself from tearing in two.

The water washed away some of the pain, enough that she could manage to soap herself and shampoo her hair. But even after a long rinse and a brisk toweling the hurt clung to her like bits of stubborn dirt. She dried her hair and dressed. At the door that led to the lobby she stopped, opened it cautiously and peered out before leaving the safety of the locker room. But the lobby was empty and she walked through it. Before venturing onto the street she looked both ways to make sure he was nowhere around.

Lynne trudged all the way to the office, uneasy at the mere thought of standing still in a crowded bus. She craved air and movement. She was tired, but the weariness brought with it a certain amount of relief. She even walked extra blocks before stopping in a deli for juice and coffee and going into the office.

Tom was already at his desk when she arrived, engaged in his prework ritual. He arrived well beore starting time and filled in the crossword puzzle in the morning paper over a breakfast of coffee and a Danish. "G'morning," she said, not stopping by his desk to chat as she ordinarily did.

Tom waggled his pen at her and looked up from the paper, surprised to see her already closing the door to her office. He completed another corner of the puzzle and noticed some strange muffled sounds coming from Lynne's office. He debated for a moment and then went to knock on her door. "Lynne?"

Lynne took a quick pass at her eyes with the napkin that had come with her coffee. "Yes?"

"Can I come in?"

She dumped the soggy napkin in the trash can under her desk. "Door's open."

"If I'm out of line you can send me home with two feet of the slush pile tonight, but are you all right?"

Lynne managed a hoarse laugh, touched by his concern. "I'm okay. Maybe I'm coming down with the flu or something."

"There's a lot of that going around. Maybe you should take the day off," he suggested.

"Too much to do," she said, gesturing to the piles of papers and manuscripts on her desk.

"Can I get you something?"

"No, thanks." He was being so sweet that it nearly brought on another round of tears. "Just close the door when you go out," she said gently.

Flu, my Aunt Sally, Tom thought as he returned to his desk. It was Tuesday morning. Something must have happened between her and the squash guy. Tom polished off the puzzle, drained his coffee container and rolled a sheet of paper into the typewriter. *Men and women sure do mess each other up*, he decided as he banged out the first reply in the pile of rejection letters he had promised himself to finish this morning. He had completed three when Lynne's door opened. She was wearing her coat and carrying a briefcase jammed with manuscripts.

"I'm going to take your advice," she said. "Go home and read in bed. Don't refer any calls unless it's urgent. I mean really urgent, Tom."

"Got it. I hope you feel better," he said kindly.

"So do I," Lynne mumbled.

JOSH HAD RIDDEN the subway into Brooklyn before he realized that the car was nearly empty and that he had missed his stop. He hadn't even noticed the crowd thinning as they passed the lower Manhattan stops that serviced the thousands of office buildings in the Wall Street area. Just as the doors were about to close he hurried out of the car and crossed the platform to wait for a train going in the opposite direction. *I don't know if I'm coming or going,* he said to himself as he waited impatiently for a train.

He buried his nose in the *Wall Street Journal*, but the facts and figures danced by him like a crowd of unruly schoolchildren. They scrambled here and there, shouting and colliding, pushing and shoving. Try as he might he couldn't get them to behave.

Josh finally crammed the newspaper into his briefcase and looked down into the tunnel for an oncoming train. Far, far away he spotted a pinpoint of light. The light at the end of the tunnel, he thought, a giddy moment of renewed hope settling over his grimness. But behind the light a rickety, graffiti-smeared subway train hobbled into the station. He got into a car and let it carry him back in the same unsatisfactory direction from which he had come.

10

WHEN SHE GOT HOME, Lynne undressed, put on her bathrobe and made a pot of tea, cosseting herself as if she really did have the flu. *I couldn't feel any worse if I did,* she thought as she climbed back into bed and surrounded herself with a stack of manuscripts, fully intending to lose herself in their pages. One of the reasons she loved working with books was their power to absorb her attention, engage her mind and renew her spirits, no matter how low she felt.

She sipped from her mug of Earl Grey tea and picked up the first manuscript in the pile with the slight charge of anticipation she always felt when considering something new. But the little electrical sensation died when she read the title: *The Pet Workout Book*. An exercise book for dogs and cats? Lynne leafed through it desultorily. The pet market was a big one, but she couldn't imagine that more than a dozen of even the most-enthusiastic pet owners would want to know how to teach their dogs to play basketball. She scrawled "No, thank you, insufficient market," on the cover letter, so that Tom would know which of her standard rejection letters should accompany the manuscript back to its agent.

By noon she had worked her way through half a dozen book proposals, but the release she sought in reading did not come. She got out of bed and moved restlessly around the apartment, ending up in the kitchen to heat a can of soup. She sat at her small table to eat it, salting it with tears and finally pushing away the half-eaten cold bowl.

In midafternoon she dressed and went out for a walk, winding her way to Carl Schurz Park, which she found empty but for a few elderly men and one or two women with young children. She stared out over the East River for a long while, snuffling into a crumpled tissue she found in her pocket. The park was built over the FDR Drive and below her cars zoomed up and down the highway. To the south she watched tiny cars move busily over the Queensboro Bridge, and envied everyone who had somewhere to go. Only when her teeth began to chatter from standing still so long in the cold November air did she take another leisurely route back to her apartment.

She frittered away the rest of the day reading more manuscripts, writing some letters, grilling a cheese sandwich that she didn't want and couldn't eat. Finally she turned on the television and waited for the flickering images to dull the edges of the pain.

When the phone rang, Lynne's mind jumped immediately to Josh. *Let it be him*, she prayed, crossing the room to answer the call. She didn't realize how hoarse her voice was or how stuffy her head until she tried to say hello. Her first attempt was a mere croak; her second managed to make contact with the caller.

"You sound terrible," a female voice said. With a sinking feeling Lynne recognized it as Jenny's. Lynne said nothing.

"It's Jenny," her caller said after a pause.

Just Friends

"I know," Lynne answered dully.

"Are you all right?"

"Flu."

"Oh, no," Jenny cooed. "I called to see if you were free for dinner. I'm right around the corner—I had to come uptown to meet someone. You sound like you could use some cheering up. Why don't I come over?"

Seeing Jenny Howard was the last thing Lynne needed right now. "Don't bother," she said curtly.

"It's no bother. What are friends for?"

What indeed, Lynne wondered bitterly.

"Do you need anything?" Jenny continued, thinking that Lynne sounded very cranky. Well, some people were like that when they get sick. "Milk, juice, tissues?"

"Nothing." Lynne realized she was holding the phone so tightly her knuckles were white. With effort she relaxed her grip.

"How about a treat? Ice cream, chocolate cake?" Jenny coaxed.

"No," Lynne replied sharply. "I don't need anything."

"You sound as grouchy as an old bear," Jenny retorted. Sick was one thing, but rude was something else, she said to herself. But almost before the thought was finished Jenny started to feel guilty. Things were touchy enough between her and Lynne without her flying off the handle because Lynne was sick and crabby. She softened her tone. "I know how you feel, though. I get very cross when I'm sick, too. I'm going to pick up some treats and bring them over—whether you like it or not," she clucked in her best mother-hen fashion. "I'll be there in about ten minutes. I'll ring twice so you'll know it's me." Jenny hung up without giving Lynne a chance to say no.

What do I do now, Lynne thought gloomily. She couldn't very well not answer the bell. Jenny'd think she'd passed out or something and call an ambulance. Shuffling listlessly, Lynne went into the study to wait for Jenny to buzz.

JENNY STOPPED IN A BAKERY on Second Avenue for a box of delicate butter cookies, and in the liquor store two doors away for a small bottle of brandy, wondering if she was doing the right thing. Sometimes when you were sick you didn't want to see anyone—even friends. She shrugged off the notion. Lynne was just being stubborn, as she could be now and then. She and Josh had even talked about it on Saturday night when they'd run into each other unexpectedly at a cocktail party at the Society for Financial Management. Still, she couldn't ignore the fact that there had been a distinct chill in her relationship with Lynne lately. Ever since Lynne had introduced her to Josh. Not for the first time it occurred to Jenny that Lynne might be jealous, but knowing the idea was absurd she dismissed it with an uneasy laugh. She turned onto Lynne's street, found her building and pressed the buzzer for two long rings.

"I'm not deaf," Lynne muttered, as she rose to answer Jenny's summons. She waited for the knock—and some time after it—before answering the door.

She was certainly taking her time, Jenny grumbled to herself as she waited, but when she saw Lynne—her eyes puffy and bloodshot, her nose a bright radish red—her annoyance melted into sympathy. "You poor thing," she cried.

I can't look that bad, Lynne thought, raising a hand to her hair. *Except in comparison to you.* Jenny was looking especially lovely in a periwinkle blue cloche and a trim overcoat in a darker shade of blue. Just what she needed right now, Lynne decided with a grimace. She looked like something out of a cold medicine commercial and Jenny looked as if she'd just finished shooting a cover for *Glamour*.

Jenny held out the brown paper bag that held the brandy bottle. "I've got some 'medicine' here. It won't cure you, but after a couple of snorts you won't be able to feel whatever's wrong." She waggled the cookie box in her other hand. "And a spoonful of sugar to make the medicine go down."

"You shouldn't have bothered with all this, Jenny," Lynne said coldly. Although she needed coddling it was impossible to accept it—even ungraciously—from Jenny.

"But I did. So you might as well go and curl up on the couch and enjoy it." She shooed Lynne into the living room and got a couple of glasses and a plate for the cookies from the kitchen.

Obediently Lynne went into the other room, having decided that the best thing to do was to let Jenny chat to her for ten or fifteen minutes and then to say she was feeling very sleepy and ask her to leave.

Jenny came in with the brandy and cookies and settled herself on the couch near Lynne.

"I wouldn't get too close," Lynne said, making her voice sound more hoarse than it actually was and backing into the corner of the couch. "I could be contagious." Wickedly she wished that she really was sick and could pass the germs to Jenny. But as far as she knew nobody had ever caught a broken heart from being with someone who had one.

She seems to want to get as far away from me as possible, Jenny thought, watching Lynne cling to the arm of the sofa as if it were a life raft. She poured the brandy and offered Lynne a cookie from the plate. Lynne shook her head.

"Refusing food?" Jenny said with forced lightness. "You really must be sick." She expected at least a feeble chuckle from Lynne but got no response. "Have you seen a doctor?"

"No."

"I hope you didn't go to work today."

"Came home early," Lynne croaked.

"Did you manage to get some sleep?" Lynne's face was growing stonier by the second, and Jenny felt as if she'd been dropped into a wide river and was swimming against the current.

"A little."

Lynne had not picked up her brandy. "Would you rather have some juice or tea or some water?" Jenny asked solicitously, though her patience was growing very short. "You should drink a lot of fluids or you'll get dehydrated. Shall I get you something?" The current seemed to be getting stronger by the minute.

"I don't need to be fussed over, Jenny."

The tone of Lynne's voice was forceful enough to wash her up over the rocks. "Excuse me," Jenny said, not hiding her hurt. "I was only trying to help."

"I didn't ask you to come here." Lynne glanced away. She knew she was being unfair to Jenny, but she couldn't seem to help herself.

Just Friends

Instead of returning that sharp shot with one of her own, Jenny took a long pull on her brandy. When she felt a measure of composure she said evenly, "Just what is going on here, Lynne? Are you angry with me for something?" Lynne's look more than answered the question. "Would you mind telling me what it is?" she asked with saccharine sarcasm.

"Come off it Jenny. I know you're not the blue-eyed innocent you appear to be."

The thought that Lynne was jealous shot once more to the surface. And the whole situation—she and Lynne eyeing each other like two suspicious cats waiting to chase the same mouse, each waiting for the other to make the first move—struck her as not only absurd but lamentable. And laughable. Like a scene in a French farce.

Angry tears sprang to Lynne's eyes at the sound of Jenny's laughter. "What's so funny?" Nothing, but nothing made her more furious than being made to look foolish.

"Lynne," Jenny said dismissively, "you couldn't possibly be jealous—about Josh, I mean." She laughed again, expecting Lynne to join in now that she'd put her crazy idea out in the open. But she was wrong.

"Couldn't I?" Lynne accused.

Jenny sobered quickly. "What you couldn't be is more wrong. I've hardly seen him."

"You saw him Saturday night, didn't you?"

"Well, yes, but I only met him by—"

"He came running to you and told you all about what's been going on between us."

"He did mention that—" Jenny began, but Lynne broke in even more insistently than before.

"You needn't—"

"You could let me finish a sentence," Jenny interrupted angrily. "If you did you might see what's going on."

"I'm not interested in your explanations," Lynne put in sharply. "Go somewhere else to soothe your conscience."

"Did it ever occur to you, Lynne," Jenny answered, controlling her fury with great difficulty, "that I don't have anything on my conscience that needs soothing?"

Lynne gave Jenny a lethal glare. "I knew you were cool, Howard, as unflappable as they come, but I didn't think you'd stab a friend in the back."

Jenny rose and grabbed for her coat and hat. If she didn't go now she was going to throttle Lynne. "That does it, Farrell. You are the most incredibly stubborn, pigheaded so-and-so I have ever known."

"I know that's what you think about me. You managed to convince Josh of it, too," Lynne charged bitterly.

"He didn't need any help from me." Jenny crammed her hat on her head and started for the door. "If you ever cool off enough to listen to what someone else has to say, give me a call. If you catch me on a really good day I might even talk to you."

"Take the stuff you brought with you. I don't need any guilt offerings lying around."

Jenny stopped in her tracks and looked Lynne full in the face. "Why don't you just throw them away? The way you've thrown away our friendship."

Somehow Lynne held herself together until she heard the apartment door slam. Then she buried her head in the cushions and sobbed until she cried herself into an exhausted sleep.

She woke in the middle of the night, cramped and aching. The apartment was ominously silent. The lights were still burning brightly and Lynne blinked her heavy eyes against their glare. She wanted it to be dark to match the condition of her soul.

When she sat up the first thing Lynne saw was the plate of cookies and the two glasses of brandy. She took the tray into the kitchen and poured the brandy slowly down the kitchen sink. She was about to drop the cookies in the garbage but couldn't, not with Jenny's parting shot still ringing in her ears. The box was still on the counter and she put the cookies back into it and placed it in the freezer. Somebody, she thought as she shut the freezer door, should invent a deep freeze for feelings. A handy compartment where you could numb them, store them and thaw them out when you could handle them again.

Lynne splashed her face with cold water and crawled into bed, certain that she never wanted to feel anything ever again. If you couldn't feel anything, you couldn't be hurt.

11

Lynne awakened groggily to the alarm the next morning. Her head ached, her mouth was dry, and for a moment she couldn't figure out why she felt so bad. But as the fog in her head cleared both of the previous day's ghastly scenes crowded in on her. She was tempted to bury herself under the covers and not come out, but she rose resolutely, dressed and went to work. One day of self-indulgence had been quite enough. Sitting around moping would only make her feel worse. Keeping busy was what she needed.

At the office she attacked the day's work with vigor. She put in several phone calls to agents she'd been meaning to see; went to the editorial meeting; wrote a long memo to the publicity director about several of her projects. She ordered in a sandwich for lunch and didn't stop working while she ate. On her way to see the art director in midafternoon she dropped another pile of things to do on Tom's desk.

Tom covered his face in mock despair. "More? What turned you into the human dynamo today?"

"Spring cleaning," Lynne declared.

"Lynne, it's November."

"Nothing like getting a head start on a job," she said and walked briskly down the hall.

She worked on purposefully until the end of the day, and then continued long after Tom had gone and her colleagues had waved good-night on their way out of the office. She didn't realize how late it was until she heard the sounds of trash baskets being emptied and the hum of a vacuum cleaner. The cleaning crew had arrived. She looked at her watch—it was seven forty-five. *Can't stay here all night,* she told herself as she put on her coat and hat. Even though that was exactly what she would like to have done. She had no desire to go home, but as she walked slowly to the elevator she realized that she was quite tired and even a little hungry.

She took as long as she could getting home, dawdling at the grocery store, looking in shop windows, walking with slow measured steps, climbing the stairs carefully instead of bounding up them as she usually did. The apartment was just as cold and silent as she had feared and before even taking off her coat she switched on the radio and filled the rooms with music, as if the sound waves could chase away the chill that pervaded the air.

She changed out of her suit and silk blouse into jeans and a sweat shirt, then went into the kitchen to make an omelet and a small salad. She poured herself a glass of red wine and sipped it as she prepared her meal, as was her custom. Usually she liked coming home at the end of a hard day for a quiet dinner by herself. It gave her time to reflect on the day, to think about tomorrow, to relax in her own rhythm and space. But tonight her internal rhythm was out of sync, alternately jumpy and sluggish; there was too much space allowing too much thought.

It wasn't this bad at the office, she muttered silently as she set her place at the table. She had worked so hard she hadn't the time to think about anything but accomplishing each task set out in front of her. There was no reason the same strategy wouldn't work at home. She got a pad and pen from her desk and as she picked at her dinner made a list of things she needed or wanted to do. Not only were there a score of home improvements she had been meaning to find time for, there was a whole enormous pulsating city out there, throbbing with things to see and do and new people to meet.

FROM A NOTICE on the bulletin board of the squash club, Lynne found a new partner—a woman— and arranged to play a couple of games a week after work. There was no chance of running into Josh then because his schedule was less flexible than hers and mornings before work were the only sure times he could get to a game.

She signed up for a lecture series on Chinese painting at the Metropolitan Museum of Art and a Saturday-morning course on darkroom techniques. She'd always wanted to see more of the art in New York's hundreds of galleries, and decided to dedicate Saturday afternoons to exploring Fifty-seventh Street or Madison Avenue or Soho. Her home-improvement projects included expanding the storage space in the kitchen, painting the living room and redecorating the bedroom. Surrounded by projects like a sick child with a bed full of stuffed animals, she would have a buttress against loneliness.

She embarked on her new program with determination, parceling out her time in order to fit everything in, and was surprised to find in a few weeks that her plan was working. Her new squash partner was faster and younger than she and their games were challenging, forcing Lynne to rely on strategy and experience to overcome her opponent's advantages. Knowing how to develop her own pictures gave her a sense of being in control, at least of her camera. Making her small dark bedroom into a warm and cozy place taxed her ingenuity. She scoured the cluttered, hole-in-the-wall fabric shops of the lower East Side on two successive Sunday mornings to find just the right materials for a bedspread and pillow shams.

She made a couple of acquaintances: an actress in the darkroom class, and a very interesting lawyer in the lecture series who had his own small practice in maritime law. They went out for coffee a couple of times after the lectures, and although Lynne was not interested in rushing into anything, she thought it not inconceivable that they might begin dating at some point in the future.

At work she negotiated two very shrewd book deals in one week and finally won the respect of the new editor in chief, whom she knew had doubted her ability to keep up with the faster, more-competitive pace he had set at Parker and Hamilton.

She was feeling good about herself again; her wounds had healed. The scars were there, but even they were becoming smoother and less visible.

On the first Saturday in December, Lynne woke up full of energy, pulled on jeans and a pretty electric-blue sweater and walked through Central Park to her darkroom class, held at a private school on the West Side. It was a perfect winter day: a blue-white sky as clear as ice, pale yellow sunshine warming the still-soft ground, the last few autumn leaves crunching under her feet as she strode along the park pathways.

After the class she and her actress friend took the subway downtown to Soho and had lunch in a bar on Prince Street that grilled great hamburgers. They spent the rest of the afternoon wandering in and out of the galleries and shops that had turned a nearly deserted factory-and-warehouse district into one of the city's most expensive and exclusive neighborhoods.

On the subway home Lynne mulled over the possibilities for the evening. She had purposely not made any plans, for an unplanned Saturday night was a great challenge. There were a couple of movies she wanted to see, or maybe she'd order in some Chinese food and spend the evening with a new mystery. In the apartment she dropped her camera bag on her desk and was on the way into the kitchen to make a cup of tea when she noticed there was something scribbled lightly in pencil on that day's square on her wall calendar.

Must be some note to remind myself to do something, she thought as she bent closer to read the untidy scrawl. "Primavera. Alice Tully. 8:00 P.M." Suddenly she remembered the two tickets sitting in the desk drawer. She'd bought them months ago and must have forgotten to make the entry in her daily diary. This calendar, with its beautiful reproductions of a series of woodcuts by the American impressionist Mary Cassatt, was hung over the desk for aesthetic reasons, not to keep track of her appointments and activities. The Primavera Quartet was one of her favorite chamber-music ensembles. She couldn't imagine how she had forgotten not only to mark the entry in her diary but about the concert itself.

The reason for her lapse of memory appeared like

an uninvited, unexpected and unwanted guest at the door. She'd bought the tickets in order to ask Josh to the performance. It was after that night that they'd listened to the Primavera's record in his apartment and he'd said he'd never heard them live. Her composure began to break, but she slammed the door firmly on the intruder. It was all very simple, really. She'd make a cup of tea and then she'd get on the phone and find someone else to use the second ticket.

Mug in hand, Lynne started calling friends. She reached more answering machines and ringing phones than people, and those few who were in already had plans for the evening. By the time she got to the last page of her address book her half-finished tea was stone cold, and she still hadn't found anyone who could attend the concert with her. She toyed briefly with calling the maritime lawyer. She knew he lived in the West Nineties, but they hadn't exchanged phone numbers and calling at this late hour would be too forward.

After a few moments in thought she came up with one other person to call—Tom Doran. She looked up his home number and dialed, but was a bit thrown by the crisp British-accented voice that answered the phone, "Mr. Doran's residence."

Quickly she realized it was Tom pretending to be his own butler. Smiling to herself she put on her best formal tone. "This is Miss Farrell. Is Mr. Doran available?"

"That depends, madam."

"On what, may I inquire?"

"On what he is wished to be available for. My apologies, madam, for ending a sentence with a preposition. It is a situation up with which you are loath to put." Tom's accent fell apart with a giggle. "How ya doing, Lynne?" he asked in his normal voice.

"I'm okay, but what have you been drinking?"

"Nothing. Just been watching an old movie on TV, *Ruggles of Red Gap*. Charles Laughton plays this British butler stranded in the Wild West. It's a riot."

"I know. I've seen it," Lynne said.

"You're not calling from the office, are you? If you are I'm hanging up."

"That zealous I'm not," she replied with a laugh. "This is a social call."

"Why Miss Farrell, I never imagined...." Tom switched to a deep Southern drawl.

"All the people in New York," Lynne intoned dryly, "and I had to call the 'man of a thousand voices.'" She told him why she was calling.

"Gee, I'd love to, but I've got what is known in the vernacular as a 'hot date.'"

They chatted for a few more minutes. "Well, I'll let you get back to your movie," Lynne said. "Have a good time tonight."

"You, too. See you Monday."

Lynne put down the phone with a sigh. Well, maybe one of the answering-machine owners would call back. She made herself a sandwich and settled down with the current issue of *The New Yorker*, leafing through for the cartoons first, then reading the book and film reviews. Her phone was all too silent, and at seven o'clock she showered and dressed and caught the bus, or buses, as it was necessary to transfer to get to Lincoln Center from her apartment.

She got off the crosstown bus and joined the stream of people, including many of her fellow riders, on their way to events at Lincoln Center: the Metropolitan Opera company, or the New York Philharmonic at Avery Fisher Hall, or the City Ballet at the New York State Theater. Alice Tully Hall—the smallest of the center's music halls, designed for chamber ensembles and solo recitals—was only a short block from the bus stop. It was outside the main complex and adjoined the Juilliard School of music. As she approached the glass doors of the hall, she saw a very thin young man, violin case and pale skin identifying him as a music student, standing near the doors, asking if anyone had an extra ticket to the sold-out performance. Lynne had rarely attended a concert in New York where someone was not trying to buy or sell tickets outside the hall, but she'd never before had an opportunity to join in the practice.

The young man offered to pay her for the ticket, but he looked like he could better spend the money on a good meal, and she refused his money. He thanked her profusely and they entered the hall together. It took some coaxing, but Lynne managed to get him to talk a little. He was—as she had suspected—a violin student at Juilliard, in his first semester, in New York for the first time from his home in Michigan. He asked her no questions and seemed relieved when Lynne opened her program.

She glanced at a list of the selections to be played and then turned to the program notes on them, but her mind strayed from what she was reading. This was not the evening alone she would have chosen. It put her in too close proximity with the past. She couldn't stop thinking about that evening in Josh's apartment—listening to music with him, cooking a meal together. Although the violin student was occupying the seat beside her, she felt Josh's absence strongly. Actually it was more his presence that she felt, as if he was there in the concert hall with her. She was relieved when the lights dimmed and the musicians took the stage—four very young, very attractive women wearing long flowing dresses of the same design in complementary spring colors. Their appearance, as well as their music, had the freshness, the promise of spring—*la primavera* in Italian.

By the end of the first half of the program some of the sense of freshness and promise Lynne had felt that morning had been restored. She had come to a concert she'd intended to attend with Josh and made it through the first half without disaster. But for a few lurking thoughts it had been a pleasant evening so far. It was difficult to be morose when surrounded by so much clear beautiful sound, and Lynne applauded enthusiastically with the rest of the crowd as the quartet left the stage.

When the lights went up the music student bolted from his seat. Probably so he wouldn't have to go through the ordeal of talking to her again, Lynne surmised. Leaving her coat and scarf in her seat, she filed out of the auditorium into the small lobby and stood near the side wall. For a while she surveyed the crowd, looking for interesting faces and trying to guess people's occupations from their dress and manner. But she quickly tired of playing the game alone—her clever, silly or astute observations went unheard, unappreciated.

The room was becoming uncomfortably smoky

and Lynne decided to make her way to the water fountain and then back into the hall. As she moved around the knot of people she had been standing behind she caught a glimpse of dark curly hair that reminded her of Josh's. *Stop being dopey,* she told herself curtly and looked away. *He's not in this hall; he's probably miles away.* But she couldn't resist glancing again in the direction of the shiny dark curls.

JOSH SIMMONS WAS ONLY half listening to what Jenny Howard was saying about the concert. He was looking around the room, hoping for a glimpse of swinging auburn hair. For just a second he thought he saw just that when a group of people standing by the far wall shifted. But he told himself to cut it out. The chance that Lynne was there was slimmer than Jane Fonda after a workout.

"You haven't heard a word I've said, Josh," Jenny was saying.

He looked down at her fondly. She'd been a good friend to him after the disastrous fight with Lynne, which was not so surprising because she was nursing similar wounds. He gave her a casual pat on the shoulder. "Sorry, Jenny. Woolgathering."

"You must have gotten enough for a sweater or two. You were miles away."

"What were you saying?"

Jenny repeated her comment about the performance—this time in Finnish. Josh gave her an absentminded "Uh-huh." Then she felt his hand tighten on her shoulder.

NEVER LOOK BACK, the old adage went. Lynne cursed herself for not following it. The black curls did belong to Josh. She stood frozen for a long second, her eyes darting around like those of a trapped animal looking for an escape route. But by then Josh had spotted her, his eyes cutting a smooth swath across the crowded smoky room. Bravely she held his glance, willing herself not to bolt, reminding herself that she was a grown woman not a scared little rabbit.

She saw in his eyes a mixture of the same things that must have shone from hers: defiance, hurt, longing, pride. But the hurt in hers grew when she saw that his hand was on Jenny's shoulder. She turned decisively on her heel when she heard him call her name. She continued walking, but a man touched her elbow.

"I think someone is calling you, miss," he said helpfully.

"Thank you," she answered politely, not feeling in the least grateful. The delay had allowed Josh just enough time to catch up with her.

"Hello, Lynne," he said softly.

"Josh." She looked squarely at his chin, unable to meet his eyes, unwilling to look at the rest of his body and be reminded of how the arms had held her, how the strong chest had felt pressed against hers.

"How have you been?"

"Fine," she replied. "And you?"

"Okay."

She held herself rigid, torn between running away and hugging him. His arms moved slightly toward her and for a bewitching bothersome moment she thought they were about to enclose her, but they fell stiffly to his side once more.

Just Friends   165

"Enjoying the concert?" Josh hadn't felt so awkward since the year in junior-high when he discovered that girls were not an alien race but full-fledged and valuable members of the same species.

Jenny had stayed behind when Josh dashed away, but after watching him with Lynne for a few painful minutes she thought they needed to be rescued. Not that it would endear her any to Lynne, she knew, being here with Josh, even though the circumstances were just as innocent as they had always been.

"Hello, Lynne," Jenny said with a friendly smile.

Despite herself Lynne was glad to see Jenny—and not only because her arrival had ended the painful encounter with Josh. But then Josh touched Jenny's wrist—lightly and for a fraction of a second. It was enough to remind her that her two "friends" were here at the concert together, and she was alone. "Hello," she said stonily.

So that's how the land lies, Jenny thought to herself. She gave Josh a puzzled glance, wondering why he'd chosen that moment to touch her, unless it was for reassurance. "Lovely concert, isn't it?" she asked a little sadly, feeling like she was in one of those pictures for children that appear in newspapers and magazines, headed, "What's Wrong with This Picture?" Someone usually had his shoes on the wrong feet or a drawer was opening upside down. The problem was obvious, but unlike the children's drawing, there was nothing she could do to solve it.

"Yes," Lynne replied, suddenly feeling sad and very, very tired. She was casting about for something to say when the lobby lights blinked. People began shuffling back to their seats, but Lynne, Josh and Jenny remained in their awkward triangle. "I guess we'd better go back in," Lynne said finally. The crowd was moving past them like water around a rock.

"Yes," Josh agreed, though he was reluctant to leave. There was so much to say, but none of it could be said in a public place.

"Goodbye," Lynne said, including them both with a short nod. She stepped into the moving current of people to let herself be propelled back into the auditorium.

As she passed Josh she heard him say in a choked voice, "It was good to see you."

For the second time that night she looked back but couldn't tell if he had meant what he said or if he had spoken sarcastically.

Lynne sat through the rest of the concert numbly, hearing only the broad outlines of the music, missing the subtleties, the nuances. As soon as the final piece was over she left the hall, not waiting to applaud or listen to the encores that were sure to come. She hailed a cab on Broadway and had the driver drop her off on Second Avenue, several blocks from her apartment. She wanted some air and a walk before she reached home.

All her hard weeks of self-improvement, self-discipline had been undone in two short minutes. Now she would have to start all over, take a refresher course in forgetting. Although the material would be familiar, this time around Lynne suspected the lesson would be no easier to learn.

She stopped at a newsstand to buy the early edition of the Sunday paper and passed the tiny shop that sold freshly made bagels. The smell of the baking rolls reminded her of her skimpy supper. She joined the long line inside the shop. When she reached the counter she asked for one onion bagel.

"What else?" the counterman asked, flapping open a paper bag and poising his hand above the bins of fresh round rolls that came covered with onion flakes or sesame seeds or poppy seeds or coarse kosher salt.

"That's all," she said.

"You just want one bagel, lady?"

"Just one."

He shrugged, tossed the bagel in the bag and handed it to her. It weighed almost nothing. The loneliness she carried with her was heavier by far.

12

"She's not in the ladies' room," Jenny announced to Josh, who was standing in the nearly deserted Tully Hall lobby. "She must have slipped out before the encores." They had rushed out of the auditorium right after the encores and stationed themselves by the door through which Lynne would exit the hall, intending to ask her to join them for a drink. But she had never appeared.

"I'll just have one more look inside," Josh said. But the only people in the auditorium were a couple of ushers and a stagehand removing chairs and music stands from the stage. "Come on," he said gruffly to Jenny. "I'll take you downtown."

"You don't have to, Josh. I can get a cab."

"Don't feel like going home," he said, holding open the door for her. "So much for 'the best laid schemes o' mice and men,'" he said, quoting Robert Burns.

"Come on, Josh. She had no way of knowing we were going to ask her to come for a drink with us. I'd probably have done the same thing in her situation. It couldn't have looked good—the two of us together and you touching me all the time."

A taxi slammed to a halt beside them and Josh helped Jenny into it. "Was I touching you?" Josh asked, looking slightly puzzled.

"Only in the friendliest way," Jenny replied,

reaching for the strap at the side of the cab as it jolted forward. "But those sorts of signals are easy to misread."

"For an editor, she sure does a lot of misreading."

"Maybe it's the way the material is presented," Jenny said, giving Lynne the benefit of the doubt.

Josh was silent as the cab tore down Broadway. Over the weeks his anger at Lynne had diminished, replaced by a hollow longing. He missed her—pure and simple. He missed playing squash with her, he missed having breakfast with her, talking to her, joking with her, making love to her, loving her. He thought about what Jenny had just said. Maybe he hadn't presented his material properly, not forcefully or definitively enough since the moment he realized his interest in her was much more than platonic. It was something to think about. But not on an empty stomach. "Are you hungry?" he asked Jenny.

"I could eat something," she allowed. And there was no reason for her to be hurrying home alone so early on a Saturday night.

"Pizza?"

"Sounds good."

Josh leaned forward and asked the driver through the Plexiglas partition to stop at Twelfth and Broadway instead of Eighth. A few minutes later the cab pulled up in front of a cheery corner pizzeria. The place was an updated version of the classic pizza joint: the tablecloths were checkered, but in rosy pink or fern green, not red; the pizzas came to the tables in pans, but they were deep black iron skillets, not flat silver trays. The place was honest, unpretentious and served delicious pizza.

They were shown to a table in the middle of the

spacious room by a young woman with a swan's neck and the turned-out gait of a dancer. Most of the staff were dancers or actors between jobs, judging from the number of pliés and relevés that were performed while waiting for orders from the kitchen, and the number of folded scripts that stuck out of the back pockets of their white trousers.

Josh and Jenny ordered a carafe of red wine and two different individual pizzas to share—one with a topping of onions and three different cheeses, the other the house special with everything but the kitchen sink.

"So what's wrong with my presentation?" Josh asked. He sipped some wine and peered over his glass at Jenny. Neither had to clarify the subject under discussion. Whenever they'd gotten together in the past few weeks Lynne had been their principal topic of conversation.

Jenny thought for a moment before answering. "When you saw her tonight and went to talk to her it looked like you had run into someone you didn't want to see, but you had to say something because it would be impolite not to. I think you missed your chance, Josh."

"What did you expect me to do, Jen? Take her in my arms and kiss her, get my face smacked, make a big scene?"

"It might have been better. At least you'd have made your point."

"I didn't see you gushing with goodwill and pledging undying friendship," Josh countered.

"It didn't occur to me at the time. Besides, you're the one with the real problem. My symptoms are only a side effect. Get to the real cause and they'll disappear."

Just Friends

Their food was served and they ate quietly for a few moments. Josh looked across the table at Jenny. As much as he liked her and enjoyed being with her, he wished he could shut his eyes and make her dematerialize—as they did on "Star Trek." *Beam down Farrell*, he would say to the engineer, Mr. Scott. *Right away, Captain*, Scotty would answer. And there she would be in a twinkling, tucking into her pizza with that truck-driver's appetite.

"Josh, you're wearing the goofiest smile I've ever seen."

Josh verbalized his silly fantasy and Jenny grinned indulgently. "Thanks a lot, Simmons. You really know how to make a girl feel wanted."

Josh's face fell. "That's just the problem—I don't."

"Come off it, Josh. You haven't even tried, have you?"

He shrugged, knowing that Jenny was right. "You know how it is, Jenny. Pride is tough to swallow."

"Pretend it's pizza," she advised.

Josh took a bite and chewed slowly. "Not bad," he said. "But I don't know about a whole meal. Where do I start, Jenny?"

"I do believe," she said pointedly, "that the telephone is still in use as a communication device. Readily available, operable by a child of three. Of course if you'd like to take a more primitive approach, there are always smoke signals, jungle drums—"

Josh snapped his fingers. "I've got it. How about if I just stand outside her window, beat my chest with my fists and howl?"

"You'd probably get her attention."

"Do you think it would work. The caveman approach, I mean?"

"Doing something is always better than sitting

around feeling powerless. But I don't think you should stay up all night practicing your Tarzan yells."

"Subtlety counts?"

"When pressed, most women will admit they appreciate it." She saw Josh's face cloud over. "It's also harder for a woman to make the first move. It goes against early conditioning. Although I hope those days are coming to an end," she added.

"It's not so easy for us guys, you know," Josh said defensively.

"I didn't say it was easy, I said you were used to it."

As they finished their meal the talk turned to other topics: the stock market, the economy, national and local politics. They lingered over their wine, both enjoying the camaraderie, both in no hurry to go home alone.

They were debating the merits of New York's current flamboyant mayor when a tall, sandy-haired man wearing horn-rimmed glasses stopped beside their table. "Hello, there," he said to Jenny.

For a moment Jenny couldn't place him, although he looked very familiar. Then she remembered. "Strand Book Store," she said, a beaming smile covering her face. Last Saturday morning she'd been roaming the stacks of the famous used-book store and had gotten into a discussion with the sandy-haired man as they'd both reached for the only copy of a novel by Rumer Godden, a writer whom they both felt was underrated both by popular and critical response. They'd talked for a long time, but parted without introducing themselves. Over the week Jenny had thought about him more than once, and had been planning on dropping into the Strand again sometime soon.

"I'm sorry, I never got your name," he said, extending his hand. "I'm David McGee."

Jenny introduced herself. "And this is my friend, Josh Simmons." Noting Jenny's accent on the word *friend*, Josh rose and shook David McGee's hand.

"We've just been up to Lincoln Center to hear some chamber music," Jenny said, to keep the conversation going.

"At Tully Hall? That's funny. My colleague and I—" he pointed to a man sitting alone at a table by the window "—were at the opera. It was Berlioz's *Faust* tonight."

"Would you excuse me for a minute?" Josh said politely and left the table. As he moved away he got a grateful glance from Jenny.

"I didn't mean to interrupt," David McGee said, watching Josh doubtfully.

"You didn't," Jenny assured him.

"I was hoping I'd run into you again sometime. I've been kicking myself all week for not getting your number."

"You can get it now," Jenny replied, reaching into her purse. "Here's my card." She scribbled her home phone number on the back.

David McGee took the card and put it in the inside pocket of his brown tweed jacket. "Is it all right if I call you?"

"Yes."

"Honestly?" he asked, casting a glance in the direction of Josh's empty chair.

"He's a very good friend," Jenny said softly. "But that's all."

"Then I will. Call you, I mean."

"I'll look forward to it."

He said good-night, gave her a smile that sealed his promise and returned to his table. Jenny sipped the last of her wine, congratulating herself for handling the encounter so coolly when her heart was racing like an overheated engine.

Josh watched from the bar, waiting until McGee left the table. On his way back to Jenny he asked their waitress for the check. Josh and Jenny split the tab and she waved to David McGee as they left the restaurant.

"Thanks, Josh," she told him. "You're a real pal."

"It was getting a little crowded around that table. I felt like I was wearing a football shirt with a big number three on it."

Jenny laughed appreciatively. "You're terrific, Josh. You'll make some woman a wonderful husband."

"I sure hope so, Jenny."

With a warm hug he left Jenny at the door of her high-rise building and rounded the corner to walk a bit before catching a cab home. He jammed his hands in the pocket of his coat and headed east on Eighth Street, then turned north on University Place. As he passed a tavern on the corner its door opened and the sounds of voices and laughter and piano music spilled out onto the sidewalk. A couple emerged, their arms wrapped around each other's waists, laughing at a private joke. The door closed and the couple disappeared into a taxi, leaving Josh alone on the cold silent street.

He peered into the window—the lighting in the pub gave it a warm reddish glow. It was filled with people seated at small round tables and standing

Just Friends

two- or three-deep at the bar. Heads wagged in time with the piano trio; faces creased into smiles and expanded into laughter. The door opened again and before it closed Josh slipped through it. Inside he could be alone with other people, instead of alone with himself.

The tavern was steamy, almost hot, and the music and voices were louder than he had imagined when standing on the outside looking in. He made his way to the bar, ordered a mug of draft beer and leaned against the polished wooden counter, foot resting on the brass rail at the base. In front of him a man and woman, who had obviously just met, interviewed each other like experienced journalists with questions such as: what do you do, where do you come from, where did you go to school, who do you know. Behind him two women talked self-consciously about the problems women faced at work, hoping, he imagined, to attract male contention and attention.

Josh tuned out the conversations and concentrated on the music—mellow jazz that wove its way around talk without disturbing it, but with plenty of substance if you cared to listen. He followed the group through a couple of numbers, enjoying the relaxed style and easy rapport among the three players. For half an hour in the anonymity and music he found a certain solace in the illusion that he wasn't alone.

He was about to order another beer when a woman with thick dark brown waves of hair and intriguing coal-black eyes chose the space next to him to order a refill from the bartender. She looked him over boldly, considered for a moment and smiled invitingly at him. On pure reflex he smiled back and was about to say something when he realized he didn't have the slightest desire to talk to her. The woman was looking at him expectantly, waiting for him to make the next move. He put his mug on the bar and walked away.

In that moment he knew he wanted Lynne, no one else would do, and he had to find a way to make her see that. He left the bar and started walking. After the artificial summery heat of the bar, the cold air felt delightfully stingingly real. He walked briskly over to Second Avenue, intending to get a cab there, but decided to walk for a few blocks, and then a few more and a few more, until at quarter to three he was nearly home.

Tired but feeling lighthearted for the first time in weeks, he picked up a Sunday paper from an all-night newsstand and ducked into the bagel shop nearby, open this late to bake the thousands of rolls that would be demanded later this Sunday morning. He asked the counterman for an onion bagel.

"What else?" he asked, flapping open a paper bag with a practiced snap of the wrist.

"That's all."

"You just want one bagel, fella?"

Buying one bagel was like wearing a loneliness badge. In honor of his decision to put that state behind him, Josh said, "Make it two."

"Last of the big spenders," the man muttered.

Josh paid for his rolls and stepped jauntily out of the shop, feeling that the rest of today might turn out very well indeed.

13

LATER THAT MORNING, after a few hours sleep, Josh brewed himself a pot of coffee, slathered his bagels with cream cheese and sat down to think of a way to approach Lynne. Phoning was the most obvious, but so conventional. Sending flowers was a possibility, but not a very imaginative one. There were those balloon bouquets, but you could hardly walk down the street these days without seeing a delivery boy carrying one. He took a bite of bagel and hummed a thoughtful little tune as he chewed.

An image from an old-time movie slipped into his head, of a sweet-faced young man in a smart uniform and pillbox hat, delivering a singing telegram. He took a swallow of coffee, brain still whirring, and then remembered an article he had read somewhere about a couple of small companies that delivered singing telegrams. He grabbed the Manhattan Yellow Pages and found not two or three entries as he had expected, but an entire page of display ads. Not only could he get a singing telegram, he could get one delivered by a tap dancer or a belly dancer or a hula dancer, a singing sheikh, a juggler, a clown, a genie or a gorilla. A gorilla? Only in New York, he thought, shaking his head.

But the shake soon turned into a nod. He could

send Lynne a gorilla gram. That would surely get her attention. He reached for the telephone and started to dial the first number, but stopped halfway through and hung up. It was nine o'clock on a Sunday morning. Where was he going to get a gorilla at this hour? But this was New York, he reminded himself. Where anyone could get anything at any hour. He dialed again. The first two places didn't answer, but the third did.

"Loony Tunes," a gruff male voice said.

"How soon could I get a gorilla?" Josh asked eagerly.

"That depends on where the gorilla's going," the man answered.

"East Eighties near Second Avenue."

"Hold on a minute." There was a loud clunk as the man put the phone down. After a muffled exchange he came back on the line. "I could have a gorilla to the East Eighties in two hours."

"Great," Josh said.

"What would you like the gorilla to sing, sir?"

Josh thought for a moment and then dictated his order.

WHO IN THE WORLD could be ringing the doorbell at eleven-thirty on a Sunday morning, Lynne thought with irritation. They had probably rung the wrong bell. She pressed down the intercom button. "Who is it?" she said into the speaker.

"Lynne Farrell?"

"Yes?" she answered cautiously.

"I have a singing telegram for you."

"I didn't order a telegram." She had been in New

York too long to open her door to any stranger who rang the bell.

"I know that, ma'am," the voice said. "It's from—" she heard some paper rifling "—someone called Simmons, Josh Simmons."

"Hold on for a minute, will you?" Lynne asked. She raced to the living room and stuck her head out the window. *I've been drinking too much coffee—or something*, she decided. There was a gorilla standing on the doorstep. Or rather a guy in a gorilla suit. He saw her looking at him and waved. Sheepishly she waved back and signaled that she was going to let him in.

She ran back to the study and pressed the buzzer. Crazily she wished that she'd had time to comb her hair and put on some makeup and that she wasn't wearing a pair of grubby jeans and a paint-smeared sweat shirt. When she heard the gorilla on the stairs she opened the door. "Come on in."

The gorilla grunted and entered the apartment. He was carrying a guitar case in one hand and a banana in the other. He put the case down on the floor.

I can't believe this, Lynne thought to herself. *I just let a strange gorilla into my apartment.* "Would you like to sit down?"

The gorilla waved no with his banana, but indicated with grunts and gestures that she should make herself comfortable. She sank into her reading chair. Her visitor took his guitar out of his case and tuned up, strumming with the tip of the banana. Lynne giggled and he did a double take, dropped the banana and unwedged a pick from between the instrument's neck and strings. In a surprisingly good baritone voice he began to sing a slow country-and-western-style ballad.

> I've acted like an ape, I've acted like a clown,
> And now it's time to stop all this monkeying around.
> I don't know how the words we said got so misconstrued,
> I never meant to say or do anything that was rude.
> I miss you, my ol' pal, I'm not handing you a line,
> And I'd like to see you soon, for some beer or for some wine.
> I wouldn't even mind getting squashed again at squash,
> I only hope you've not forgotten your good ol' buddy, Josh.

The gorilla finished singing and bowed deeply from the waist. Caught between laughter and tears, Lynne applauded the performance. "Thank you," she cried. "That was wonderful!"

The gorilla gave a bashful shrug of the shoulders.

"Did you write the lyrics?" she asked.

The gorilla shook his head and pulled a piece of paper out of the guitar case. He handed it to Lynne. It was her official Gorilla Gram, the message neatly typed in the center of a piece of light brown stationery bordered by bananas. At the bottom it said Lyrics by Josh Simmons.

Guitar in case, the gorilla was ready to leave. Lynne opened the door for him. He grunted goodbye and left her holding the banana.

Just Friends 181

WHEN THE PHONE FINALLY RANG Josh pounced on it.

"I wouldn't leave Wall Street to be a songwriter in Nashville," Lynne said.

"Oh, really?" Josh replied, a broad smile spreading across his face.

"That's the first time I ever had a gorilla come to my apartment. It was quite an experience. A real eye-opener."

"I thought it might get your attention." Josh paused. "You seemed a little remote last night."

"I'm sorry about that, Josh. I'm sorry about a lot of things," she said with a sniffle.

"Hey, hey," Josh said soothingly. He could see her so clearly in his mind's eye, defiantly fighting back tears. "I didn't do this so that we could get into a lot of hot and heavy stuff. Let's keep it light, Lynne."

She shook off the tearful feeling. "Sure, okay."

"Do you want to take a walk in the park this afternoon? It's a beautiful day."

"I'd like that."

"Shall I pick you up at two?"

"That'll be fine."

By the time she hung up, Lynne's heart was flipping and flopping like a feather in a hurricane. She leaned back in her chair and waited for the storm to subside. *Take it easy*, she told herself. *It was rushing around and making assumptions that got you into trouble before. One step at a time*, she cautioned her hasty heart. But she couldn't help feeling light and joyful all the same.

To pass the time until Josh came, Lynne tidied the apartment and then took the newspaper into the bathroom to read while she had a long soak in a hot bubble bath. Then she washed her hair until it was squeaky clean and styled it carefully with her blow dryer. She stood in front of her closet for a long time, debating what to wear before choosing her charcoal-gray pleated wool trousers and a warm popcorn-knit sweater in heathery blues and greens. Her makeup was simple—a dab of mascara, a few strokes of blusher and some lip gloss—but she applied it with surgical precision.

She had just taken her black wool jacket and a cap that matched her sweater out of the closet when the doorbell rang. Taking a few deep breaths, she walked into the study and answered the buzzer. "I'll be right down," she told Josh. She pulled her cap on at a jaunty angle, checked it in the bedroom mirror and slipped into her jacket. Her knees were so shaky going down the stairs that she had to hang on tightly to the banister.

As she came down the last half flight of stairs she could see Josh through the glass in the top half of the door. He was leaning against the tree at the front of the building, arms crossed, one leg in front of the other. Under his navy blue down jacket he was wearing a cranberry-colored turtleneck that heightened the darkness of his eyes and hair. A thrill went through Lynne at the sight of him, and she reminded herself sternly that they had a lot to talk about, a lot of things to set straight on both sides.

Lynne opened the door and stepped outside. At the sight of her, Josh straightened and dropped his arms to his sides. They stood their ground and looked at each other awkwardly, neither knowing what to say or do.

Though she would never know what possessed her at that moment, Lynne let her jaw drop, scratched at her sides and did a little gorilla dance on her doorstep, accompanied by a grunting gorilla song. Josh stared at her as if she was crazy and then burst out laughing. In another moment he joined her in the song and dance. They didn't stop until an elderly couple passed and gave them a suspicious look. Giggling like two six-year-olds, they took off down the street toward Central Park.

In the park they walked first around the reservoir, talking intermittently and not always easily about subjects that didn't touch any raw nerves. The wind blew off the water in great gusts and turned their faces a ruddy pink. They left the reservoir on the west side of the park and went on down through the Ramble, the park's most heavily wooded area, getting reacquainted slowly, cautiously.

Finally they climbed up the hill to the Belvedere Castle, a miniature gray granite structure complete with turrets and parapets. It had been built as a weather station but had been empty and neglected for many years. Now it was refurbished, in use as a lookout tower and as a center for children's activities organized by the park staff. They took the narrow staircase up to the highest turret and stepped out of the door onto a small rampart that abutted the tower. From there they looked out over the entire park.

"It's a little like standing in a canyon, isn't it?" Lynne remarked. Mountain peaks of buildings flanked the rim of the park, giving the impression that they were standing on a ledge in the middle of a natural valley, even though everything around them—the buildings, the park itself—was manmade.

"Rather grand, don't you think?" Josh quipped.

Lynne punched him lightly in the arm. In a way it felt so right, the two of them walking in the park, talking, joking, but underneath there was a wariness, as one might have walking along a dark corridor past a row of closed unmarked doors. Anything might pop out. She lapsed into silence and so did Josh.

The afternoon sun had begun to wane and the wind swept up off the expanse of the Great Lawn, which was just below them. Lynne shivered involuntarily and stuffed her hands deeper into the pockets of her jacket.

"Cold?" Josh asked. She nodded. "Then let's go. We can stop on the way back for something hot to drink."

They left the park and walked to a café on Madison Avenue where they were served large mugs of thick sweet hot chocolate topped with whipped cream and a grating of fresh nutmeg.

"I've enjoyed this afternoon, Lynne," Josh said after they'd both chased the chill away with several sips of chocolate.

"So have I, Josh, but—"

"And I want you to know that I meant everything I said in that song—even though I didn't give Ira Gershwin a run for his money."

"You haven't had much practice," Lynne said with a sad rueful smile. "And if I can help it you won't get much more. I'm sorry if I've been childish, it's just that...." She stopped short of telling him how much he meant to her and how much it had hurt to see him last night with Jenny. She was burning to ask him about her, but recalling Josh's words she held her tongue. *Keep it light, Lynne,* she counseled herself.

"What?"

"Nothing," she said with a shake of her head.

They finished their chocolate slowly and walked back toward Lynne's apartment. At the door they stopped and looked searchingly at each other for a moment, then Josh folded her gently into his arms and pressed his cheek to hers. Lynne closed her eyes and leaned against him, luxuriating in the comfort of his arms.

"What happens now, Josh?" she asked when he released her.

"Can we see each other? Take it one step at a time this time, instead of in quantum leaps?" He steeled himself against crushing her to him, kissing her deeply and fully as he so longed to do. "If you build a bridge first it's harder to fall into the chasm."

"Shall I bring my hard hat?"

"Just your squash racket. Are you game for a game next week?"

"Sure, but you'd better watch out. I've been playing with someone really good. I've got a few more moves."

Josh raised an inquiring eyebrow. "They may be nothing compared to mine," he said huskily.

"That's something we'll have to see about, isn't it?" she answered breathlessly.

His self-control nearly exhausted, Josh quickly arranged to reserve a court for Tuesday morning. He passed his palm lightly, longingly over Lynne's cheek and said good-night.

Lynne stood in the darkening street, watching Josh as he walked swiftly down the sidewalk and then disappeared around the corner. She would never understand how she had thought she could forget him by repainting the living room. He was a part of her, like paint on a wall. She offered a brief fervent prayer that this time they could make it work.

14

"Keep hittin' 'em like that," Josh taunted as he returned her first serve. "It makes you so easy to beat."

"It does, does it?" Lynne replied, smashing the ball hard and watching Josh miscalculate its trajectory.

"Just want to keep you on your toes," Josh said, correcting his path at the last moment and reaching the ball. His shot was not placed well, however, and Lynne had no trouble putting hers in a corner of the court he couldn't possibly reach.

"Looks like you're the one who needs to stretch the tootsies," she said, preparing for her second serve.

This Friday morning was the third time they'd played squash since their walk in the park a couple of Sundays ago. The first game they'd played had been tentative, cautious and polite, and Lynne had won easily. In the second they'd begun to use the moves they'd perfected with their other partners, and by the last few points the game had become exciting, but Lynne was the winner again. They had yet to play an all-out contest.

Racket poised, Lynne took measure of Josh: knees bent, weight on the balls of his feet, eyes focused, ready for play. Or so he thought. Concentrating hard, she hit a perfect service and watched with satisfaction as the ball sailed past him. Josh gave her a look that said he'd not give her that opportunity again.

And he didn't. His playing sharpened as the game progressed. He returned Lynne's best shots consistently and it became more and more difficult for her to find an opening. But she managed to stay just barely in the lead and thought she saw signs of Josh beginning to tire. She was wrong. Just at the moment when she felt he would fade, Josh began to pour it on. He moved fast, made quick turns, placed his shots impeccably and took the lead. Lynne reached deep inside for her reserve energy, but found her physical and psychological powers more depleted than she had thought. Though she fought hard she couldn't find the extra stamina to win. When the buzzer sounded Josh was the winner by two points.

"All right!" he shouted, waving his racket in the air.

Exhausted, Lynne dropped her racket and leaned over, hands on knees, panting hard.

"Looks like you owe me breakfast, Farrell," he said jubilantly through hard deep breaths.

The last two times they'd played they hadn't had a meal together afterward. A secret smile stole over Lynne's face. "What some people won't do to save a few bucks," she said, still bent over and breathing rapidly.

The next thing she felt was a playful slap on the rump. The touch of Josh's hand was like an electric charge and she started and straightened. Their eyes caught for a moment, but then both looked away almost immediately.

Josh turned and reached for his towel. "I'll meet you in the lobby," he said. *If I don't get out of here*, he thought to himself, *I'll ravish her right here on the court.* He'd been so careful with her since that day in the park, but he didn't know how much longer he could hold out without declaring himself.

"Right," Lynne answered. She was still burning from his touch and burning to touch him. Things were on an easy enough footing for them now to talk about the one subject—their relationship—they had studiously avoided. She couldn't go on in this limbo much longer.

"WELL, WELL, look who's here!" Rose glanced up from her book as Lynne and Josh entered the Apollo Coffee Shop. "You haven't been here in ages. Have you been away?"

"Something like that," Josh said. They chatted with Rose for a few minutes and then took a booth in the back of the restaurant. After giving their orders to the waiter, they both looked down at the Formica tabletop. On the same beat they lifted their heads and spoke, as if an orchestra conductor had raised his baton.

"We've got to talk," they said in perfect unison.

They stared at each other dumbfounded and then threw back their heads and laughed.

"You first," Lynne offered.

"No, you first," Josh countered.

"No, no, go ahead."

"Are we going to have an argument about this?" he teased.

"I hope not," Lynne answered, reaching into the bowl on the table that held paper packets of sugar and toothpicks. She unwrapped a toothpick, broke it unevenly and hid the two pieces in her closed hand. "Short goes first," she said, holding out her hand for Josh to choose a toothpick half. It was the short half.

Josh folded his hands on top of the table and looked directly at her. "I don't know how we got everything wrong before, but I'm willing to try again, if you are. We're good together, Lynne. Too good not to give it another shot." He paused and thought. "That's what I have to say—for starters, that is. What about you?"

"The same," she said quietly, holding back the flood of words that were pushing at her like water at a dike.

"What happened, Lynnie?"

At the sound of the endearment some of the water found a fingerhole in the dike and ended up in her eyes. "Well," she stalled, thinking for a moment, "I don't like Japanese food that much."

Josh looked puzzled for a moment and then broke into a wide grin. He was about to say something when the waiter arrived with their breakfasts.

"What I like," Lynne continued, picking up her knife and fork, "is real food—say bacon and eggs—something you can sink your teeth into." She sank her teeth into a forkful of egg.

"Why did we go to that restaurant?" Josh asked, dipping a piece of toast into the yolk of his fried egg.

"Because you wanted to."

"Me? You were the one who seemed so intrigued by it."

"Intrigued? Only in the sense that I couldn't believe how trendy it was. Minimalism isn't my style."

"I guess they have to save on food what they

spend on the decor. I don't think I ever ate from black plates before," he said with distaste.

"You call that eating? I had to have a peanut-butter sandwich before I went to bed," Lynne confessed.

"Two hamburgers," Josh said with a grin.

"Oh, Josh," Lynne said with a sigh. "Neither of us wanted to eat there and yet we let the other think we did. That's the kind of thing that gets us—gets anybody—in trouble."

"Yeah," Josh allowed. "Maybe we should make some ground rules. Number one: Never eat in restaurants where the waitresses are dressed in parachutes."

Lynne laughed so hard she nearly choked on a mouthful of toast. Josh had to reach over and pat her on the back. When she stopped laughing he took a napkin from the dispenser on the table and wiped the tears from her cheeks. "That's exactly what I was thinking that night," she finally managed to say. "What a comedy of errors. The movie, too. I knew we wouldn't like it."

"But we went anyway."

"Mostly at my instigation."

"I didn't say no," Josh reminded her. "We can't please each other by displeasing ourselves, Lynnie."

"We really did manage to do everything 'bass ackwards,' as my father would say," Lynne joked with a shake of her head.

"Only because we'd fallen head over heels...and landed wrong side up," Josh pointed out. He reached for her hand and held it securely between his palms. "I was reeling from the dinner-dance. I didn't know what had hit me."

"Me either, Josh."

"I'd always thought of you in a certain way, not a sexual way at all, and somehow it seemed wrong. Even though at the time it had seemed ever, ever so right."

Lynne felt faint at the thought of their night together, but she understood Josh's feelings, for they echoed hers. "I was afraid we'd lose what we had, the friendship. But I wanted you, too." She paused. "I was confused and I guess it did seem to you that I was taking you for granted."

"Not only for granted, but for a fool." Josh looked at her soberly. "There was Jenny, you see."

He drew a lazy finger up and down her forearm. "How wrong you were on that score, Lynnie, but there was no telling you. You're a stubborn little what'sit sometimes," he said fondly.

"Humph," she answered, knowing that she'd been caught with her hand in the cookie jar.

"I will admit that when I met her I was, uh, more than casually interested, shall we say, but it never came to anything—for either of us. Except some companionship."

"You looked awfully chummy at the concert on Saturday," Lynne said. Her doubts needed to be swept away like cobwebs in a dusty attic.

"We were mostly talking about you," Josh said pointedly. "And we were going to ask you to join us for a drink after the concert. Jenny had agreed to disappear at a strategic moment. But you did a bunk."

Lynne felt like someone who had missed her own surprise birthday party. "I left right after the last piece. Didn't stay for the encores."

Just Friends

"So we noticed," Josh replied dryly.

The waiter appeared at their table. "Are you folks finished?"

Lynne and Josh looked down at their now cold, half-eaten breakfasts. "I think so," Josh said.

"Anything wrong with the food?"

"No," Lynne answered quickly. "We just weren't very hungry this morning." While the table was being cleared she looked at her watch. "It's getting late, Josh. We'd better get going."

But once on the street they dawdled on their way to the bus stop. Half a block away Josh said, "I don't feel like going to the office. Let's play hooky. Call in sick for the day. We've got so much more to say to each other, Lynnie."

"I don't know, Josh. I've got so much to—" She interrupted herself. "On second thought," she continued as if she had a very stuffy head, "I tink I just came down wid a terriber code in my dose."

"That's the spirit," Josh exclaimed, grabbing her hand.

They returned to their respective apartments, called their offices, exchanged suits and briefcases for jeans and sneakers and met again on Second Avenue.

"This is fun already," Lynne said, feeling free-spirited as Josh took her arm and placed it through the crook of his.

"What shall we do?"

"Umm, let me see. Walk down Fifth Avenue and look at the Christmas windows?"

Josh narrowed his eyes and looked closely at her. "Really?"

"Yup. What do you want to do?"

"Walk down Fifth Avenue and look at the Christmas decorations. But let's walk down through the park. I could use a little nature this morning."

They strolled through the park, stopping at the sailing pond to recall their picnic there at summer's end.

"Remember the *True Love*?" Lynne asked.

"I'd never forget that, Lynnie," Josh answered. "Rough seas over?" He pulled her into his arms.

"I hope so," she whispered breathlessly.

His sweet and gentle kiss warmed her like a fire on a winter's evening, bringing a tingle to her toes and fingers and a flush to her face.

They continued on down the east side of the park to the zoo, passing under the Delacorte clock with its revolving, dancing animals just as it chimed ten. They watched it, enchanted, as generations of children have done.

"I feel like a kid again, Josh. Only very grown up at the same time. It's curious."

"I hear it gets more and more curious," he teased, planting a noisy kiss on her cheek and pulling her on down the path.

"What?"

"Days like this. Being together. Falling in love," he added softly.

"Is that what we're doing, Josh?"

"We've been doing it for a long time, Lynnie. We just didn't notice."

"I think we noticed. But we didn't know how to handle it. We're doing much better this time around, aren't we?"

"Much, much better," Josh assured her. "But not as well as we're going to be doing." He drew his arm around her shoulders and hugged her tightly.

Just Friends

Most of the animals were indoors for the winter, but the seals were swimming happily in their pool, diving in and out, flapping their flippers, nuzzling nose to nose on the cement rocks above the pool. Josh and Lynne stood and watched the show for a while, then as they walked on Lynne put her cold nose to Josh's for a playful Eskimo kiss.

They left the park and soon found themselves passing the Plaza Hotel. "Do you suppose we have a lot of guests today?" Lynne asked.

"Of course, my de-ah." Josh put on a posh accent. "Everyone but everyone is in town doing their Christmas shopping." He dropped the accent and lowered his voice to a lascivious whisper. "If it was three in the morning I'd kiss the stuffing out of you."

"You may if you wish," Lynne invited primly.

"Naw," Josh said. "Wouldn't want to cause more of a traffic jam than there already is."

They crossed Fifth Avenue and spent the next hour roaming through F.A.O. Schwarz, talking to enormous stuffed giraffes and bears, traveling far on a toy train and failing to beat a computer game. When they left the store Josh bought some hot chestnuts from a street vendor and they munched them on the way down to Rockefeller Center.

The big tree was up, towering over the plaza, so majestic it could not be dwarfed even by the surrounding buildings. The center walk was afire with red poinsettias and a host of wire-and-spun-glass angels blew their trumpets at either end of the walk. The ice rink was full of skaters, most of them shakily circling the periphery, a few cutting expert figures in the middle.

Josh tugged at her hand and in a few minutes Lynne found herself lacing up a pair of rented skates and joining the group going around and around the rink. Neither of them had skated for years and their ankles wobbled at first, but after a while they were gliding easily across the ice. "Take that, Peggy Fleming," she announced with a giggle.

"And John Curry," Josh added before falling flat on his keister. Laughing, Lynne held out a hand to help him up, but found herself sprawled inelegantly across him instead.

"They must have heard us," Lynne whispered.

Hungry from the fresh air and the activity and having eaten only half a breakfast, they grabbed a quick bite in a snack bar near the rink and continued on down Fifth Avenue. There was a line in front of Lord & Taylor to see the Victorian Christmas party, complete with dancing dolls dressed in fancy costumes. They stood patiently waiting for a glimpse of the elaborate display, authentic down to the last bit of lace and tiny cup and saucer. When they reached the head of the line they viewed the first window, in which the host and hostess greeted guests at the door. The next room held the tree, with piles of gaily wrapped packages and children playing beneath it. The dining-room table in the next window was spread with candies, nuts and fruit, and a flaming plum pudding graced the center. In the last window, ladies and gentlemen waltzed to a string orchestra. As Josh and Lynne moved along they made up stories about the family, about the children's gifts, about the guests at the party. They lingered at the last window, swaying in time to the music, arms wrapped around each other's waists.

"I can't wait to dance with you again," Josh whispered in her ear. Lynne's stomach bumped and lurched like a roller coaster and she let her spinning head rest on Josh's shoulder.

"Are you sure we're not moving too fast?" she asked quietly as they moved away. "I seem to remember hearing something about quantum leaps, Josh."

"The bridge is there, Lynne. Feel the ground—" he stamped his foot down hard "—firm beneath us."

"You were right before when you said I was scared of what was going on between us," she said in a small voice.

"Still scared?" Josh questioned gently.

She nodded. "And still hurting in places," she said. "It wasn't easy without you, Josh."

"They weren't the best weeks of my life, either. What did you do?"

"Got very strict with myself. I went to classes, lectures, repainted the living room, put up some shelves in the kitchen, generally worked like a demon and filled every second so I wouldn't have time to think or to hurt."

"Did it work?"

"It beat sitting around moping. I was even getting used to it—until I saw you and Jenny at the concert. It broke my concentration, so to speak. I was trying to find the strength to start again when—" Lynne turned to him and smiled "—the gorilla arrived on my doorstep. How in the world did you come up with that?"

"Sheer brilliance," Josh preened.

"I'm so glad you're modest, as well as cute," Lynne said.

"You think I'm cute?" Josh asked coyly.

"As a button." Lynne ruffled his dark curls and cuffed his head gently. *This is wonderful,* she thought, *walking and talking, being able to say whatever needs to be said, being honest with each other.* She felt her heart expanding, taking in more and more of Josh, and contracting, giving out more and more of herself.

They walked a few more blocks and crossed the street to laugh at Altman's clever "Teddy Bear's Christmas" display. Whereas the children had been wide-eyed and awed by the other windows, they were chattering away, giggling, making faces and jumping up and down in front of Altman's. The bears rode flashy motorcycles, played computer games, turned cartwheels and somersaults. Lynne felt like turning a few herself, and when they walked away from the window could hardly restrain the urge.

"That's the last of the lot," Josh said. "What shall we do now?" They ducked into Altman's warm lobby to discuss how to spend what little remained of the day. The night, Lynne had a feeling, would take care of itself.

They decided to walk on down to the end of Fifth Avenue, through Washington Square, and then have an early supper at Josh's favorite Greenwich Village Italian restaurant. The light faded as they ambled down the avenue; the brilliant winter sky paled, took on a violet tint and then darkened. They walked in companionable silence, holding hands loosely, both enjoying the slower pace after the full day.

They were among the first of the evening's diners in the restaurant and had a hearty meal of minestrone and Chicken Cacciatore, washed down with an excellent dry Chianti. They ate unhurriedly, making sure to sop up the last of the spicy sauce that covered the chicken with the crusty yeasty bread served with the meal. There was no room for dessert after the feast, but they took their time over espresso and an after-dinner liqueur.

They talked quietly but steadily throughout the meal, telling each other funny stories, relating family tales, reminiscing about school days and childhood.

"I feel so close to you," Lynne said, as she drained the last of her espresso.

"And I to you," Josh answered, taking her hand across the table, as he had intermittently throughout the evening. "But not as close as I want to be, my darling," he whispered. "Come home with me, Lynnie?"

There was no answer but yes.

15

LYNNE FELT SUDDENLY SHY when Josh opened the door of his apartment. She hesitated and hung back in the hall.

Josh looked at her, reading her like a newspaper headline. "Yeah, I know," he said. "What if it isn't like last time? What if that was just the champagne and the music and the dancing?" He cupped her chin with his hand. "And what if it's better?"

He led her into the foyer and helped her out of her jacket, letting his hands run slowly down her arms. Goose bumps rose in the places he touched. He turned her around to face him and brought his mouth down on hers, a light touch that turned into a grinding passionate kiss.

"I want you, my darling. I need you," he fairly growled when he released her. "Now. I can't wait any longer, Lynnie." He swept her up into his arms and carried her into the bedroom, depositing her on the bed like a precious parcel. He sat beside her and gazed deeply into her eyes. His need, the urgency of it, penetrated every fiber of her body.

"I'm here, Josh. Yours," she said softly. She held out her arms to him and he leaned down on her, crushing his chest to hers. He caressed her face with wonder—eyelids, bridge of the nose, hollows of the cheeks, corners of the mouth. His touch was unbearably light. Though it made her quiver with pleasure, she grasped the back of his neck and pressed his mouth to hers, needing to taste him, feel him, smell him, see him, hear him, experience him with all of her senses.

His mouth tasted of bitter coffee and sweet licorice liqueur, his lips were full and soft, his musky masculine aroma seemed to surround her like a haze. Her eyes looked into his as his tongue darted in and out of her mouth, and he took small nibbles of her lips. He groaned his pleasure, his desire. It was a small sound, yet one that shook her like thunder.

Josh pulled away from her reluctantly. "Let's get undressed," he said huskily.

They stood and without taking their eyes from each other they kicked off their shoes, pulled off sweaters, shirts, jeans, peeled away underwear and socks. "Nothing left between us now," Josh said with a grin. He pushed her down on the bed and rolled her joyously from side to side until they were both quite giddy.

"Josh, my head is spinning," Lynne pleaded. He let her go and they lay on their backs taking long breaths.

Josh propped himself up on his elbow and looked at her body: the full breasts with their dark nipples, the long torso and flat stomach, the gentle mound between her thighs. "You're unbelievably beautiful," he breathed. "I thought I had memorized your body, but now I see I haven't even begun to know it."

"It would be glad to be better acquainted," Lynne said with a breathless giggle.

"Oh, would it?" Josh pulled himself up to his

knees, humming the tune "Getting to Know You." "Now where to start?" he mused. "Top of head or tips of toes?" He chose the latter.

Lynne had never thought that her toes were very erotic, but when Josh started to nibble on them and rub the bottoms of her feet her whole body began to tingle. He nibbled and licked his way up her ankles, her calves, her knees. When he reached the insides of her thighs she had to reach down and steady herself on his shoulders.

"I need to hold on, Josh," she said dazedly. "You're sending me right into orbit."

"Exactly the desired effect," he murmured, working his way up her thigh.

When he buried his tongue deep inside her she felt as if she'd left the earth. Gravity no longer applied to her. She was floating free in a beautiful dark blue space lit by hot, brilliant, burning stars. The space was both inside her and outside her, expanding to infinity.

Josh raised himself up and poised over her quivering body. "Look at me, Lynnie," he said softly.

Lynne opened her eyes, still feeling as if she was looking at him from some very distant place. His face came into focus and she reached out to touch it. She wanted him to join her in the vast and secret place she'd just found. She ran her hand swiftly down his chest, over the taut muscles of his flat stomach and guided him slowly into her. She crushed him against her breasts and rolled over so he was underneath.

Josh lay still for a moment and let her lead the way. His breathing was shallow and his hands lay limply on her back. She pushed herself down on him; he moaned slightly and his mouth parted in a

Just Friends

half smile. She took him, released him, took him deeper, released him again. The smile widened and his eyes fluttered open. They took a long measure of each other.

"Champagne and music would have been superfluous," Josh whispered between jagged breaths. "All we need to fly is each other." He gripped her tightly and thrust hard into her.

They took off together, tumbling and whirling in space like two sky divers who knew they would not touch earth until they wanted to. They took their time, exploring distant corners of each other, going where their fancy took them, until a giant star loomed before them, beckoning, then commanding. They shot toward it faster and faster and faster, but as soon as they reached it, it exploded, sending them both into a shattering spin. Panting and gasping, they entered a slow downward spiral.

Lynne rested her head on Josh's shoulder; beneath her his heart was pounding so hard she could feel it thumping. It was an exhilarating feeling, as if he were reaching out for her from his deepest place. She rested her hand over his heart.

Josh opened his eyes, surprised to find himself in his own bedroom. Making love with Lynne, he'd felt as if he was a million miles away. He looked at the ceiling and concentrated on a hairline crack in the plaster to reorient himself. Gradually he became aware of Lynne's weight on him—gravity was in operation once more. He shifted beneath her and she raised her head. Gently he rolled her off him and raised himself up on his elbow. She was lying still, breathing evenly, her eyes closed. He let his hand brush lightly up and down her body.

Aware that Josh was looking at her, Lynne opened her eyes. He smiled sweetly at her and a feeling so deep it seemed literally to grip her heart welled up in her. She reached up and pulled his head to her breast.

They drifted off to sleep in each other's arms and slept tangled together until the morning light crept stealthily into the room. Lynne woke with the weight and warmth of Josh's arm thrown across her chest, his leg intertwined with hers. She stirred slightly and he lifted his head.

"Oh, it's you," he said groggily.

"Who were you expecting?" she asked, ruffling his tousled curls.

"You," he said with a silly smile.

Lynne looked around the room and found the clock radio on the end table on her side of the bed. It was seven-thirty, but she wasn't sure what day it was. She asked Josh.

He opened one eye. "Saturday?" He thought for a moment and nodded. "Mmm, Saturday. Means we can go back to sleep." He thought for another moment and then began to play lazily with her nearest breast. "Or not go back to sleep," he murmured, coaxing the nipple to hardness.

They made leisurely love in the pale morning light, then fell back into a deep sleep until midmorning. Josh woke first and got out of bed carefully, but Lynne was awakened soon after by his absence and the smell of fresh coffee. She lay in bed feeling a sense of luxury, as if the sheets were satin and she a royal princess restored to a long-lost throne. In a way it was true, she told herself, for the time she'd been without Josh had been like the time in the fairy tales when the princess was forced to live a hard and meager life. But this morning she felt as rich as if she had been drenched in diamonds and robed in rubies. Richer, for she knew she had found love. *That's really what the fairy tales are about,* she reflected, *losing and finding love.* She vowed to hold on tight to what had been restored to her.

Josh walked into the room, looking princely in a gray sweat suit. "The workers have been up since dawn, your highness, preparing your breakfast," he said, sitting down on the edge of the bed. He bent over and kissed her lightly. "There's a robe on the back of the bathroom door, and pancakes a la Josh will be served in the dining room forthwith."

"Forthwith maple syrup, I hope," Lynne said happily.

He pulled down the covers and tweaked a rosy breast. "With maple syrup and butter and anything else your heart desires." His face grew suddenly serious. "Last night was wonderful, Lynnie."

"For me, too, Josh."

He held her close for a long moment. "I'd better get out of here," he said huskily. "Or we'll never get any breakfast."

Lynne went into the bathroom to wash up. In the mirror over the sink she saw that her eyes were clear and bright, her skin pink and glowing. She brushed her auburn hair until it gleamed and wrapped her body—vibrant and alive with love—in Josh's terrycloth robe.

Josh had already set the table and the morning paper was lying beside the sugar bowl. From the kitchen she could hear the sizzle of pancake batter hitting the griddle and Josh's tuneless whistling as he flipped the cakes. When he heard the scrape of a chair as she sat down, he hurried out of the kitchen with a pot of coffee and poured her a cup. Lynne scanned the front page of the paper as she waited for breakfast to be served, feeling absolutely at home and content.

A minute or two later Josh proudly produced two plates stacked high with perfectly round, perfectly browned pancakes. "I'm impressed," Lynne said as he set hers down before her.

"Just one of my many talents," he said blithely. He sat down opposite her. "Sports page, please," he requested, holding out his hand. Lynne handed over the second section.

They ate slowly, trading bits of the news back and forth as the meal progressed. After breakfast, while Josh showered Lynne washed the dishes, feeling as comfortable as if she was at her own sink at home. Suddenly a brace of tears rolled down her cheeks and plopped into the sink. Home. It wasn't the color of the paint on the walls or the size of the closets—it was who was there with you. Two more large tears dropped from her eyes.

She was so lost in thought that she didn't hear Josh come into the kitchen. "Hey, what's this?" he asked, brushing away a tear with the tip of a finger. "Happy ones, I hope."

Lynne sniffed softly. "I always cry when I have to do the dishes," she teased. "Very happy," she added in a whisper.

He folded her in his arms and held her close.

They idled away the rest of the day, reading, going out for a walk, coming back to Josh's to bake a batch

Just Friends

of chocolate-chip cookies together, then devouring them with big glasses of milk while they watched a soppy old movie on television.

In the early evening they decided on the spur of the moment to hop into a cab and go down to the ticket booth at Times Square that sold half-priced tickets for that evening's theater performances. It opened in midafternoon and there usually wasn't much left close to curtain time, but they found tickets for an off-Broadway show they'd both been wanting to see. The theater was in a row of restored buildings on Forty-second Street between Ninth and Tenth Avenues that housed half a dozen off-Broadway theaters. After the show, they popped into a café across the street for a hamburger before going back to Lynne's place for the night.

With each moment they seemed to be getting closer, cementing the bonds of their friendship with a new thicker glue, but one that wouldn't have worked had those friendly bonds not existed. Their lovemaking that night was more quiet but no less rapturous for its gentleness and tenderness.

At noon on Sunday they had finished a simple breakfast and were sitting in the living room reading the paper. Lynne put down the book review and looked across at Josh. He was so serious when he read, she could almost hear his brain whirring in the quiet as he digested and analyzed the words he was taking in. She'd never noticed that before. How many things, she thought with anticipation, there were to learn about each other. But how many they already knew, she added with contentment.

"Josh?"

"Mm?"

"I think I'd like to have the rest of the day on my own," she said quietly. "Lots of thinking to do."

"For me, too," he replied, looking up at her with a fond smile. "Come here." She sidled across the couch and he took her into his arms. He held her, stroking her hair. Lynne leaned against him, listening to the steady strong beat of his heart.

It was a sound she heard long after he had gone.

16

It was the middle of the afternoon before Lynne found the courage to pick up the phone. She knew she had to call Jenny, but she'd been putting it off ever since Josh had gone. It was so much easier—and more pleasant—to sit and daydream about him, to replay the events of the past two days, to project into the future.

When Jenny picked up the phone all the speeches Lynne had so carefully rehearsed fled her mind. "It's Lynne," she blurted out. There was a short static pause, and Lynne grabbed for words. "I just called to say I was sorry, and that—"

"It's good to hear your voice," Jenny interrupted quietly, "no matter what you're going to say."

"Thanks," Lynne said. Trust Jenny to say the right thing at the right time. "I owe you an apology, and I want to pay off my debt—if you feel you can accept it," she continued. "Could we get together sometime, maybe?"

Jenny gave a low throaty laugh. "You sound like a teenager asking for his first date."

"I'm that nervous," Lynne confessed.

"But I admit we've got a lot to talk about. Why don't you come over here for supper tonight?" Jenny offered. "I had a sudden attack of domesticity this morning and there's a pot of soup simmering on the stove. Don't ask what got into me."

Lynne laughed. "How about if I bring some bread and cheese and something for dessert?"

"Sounds good. Around seven?"

"See you then."

Lynne hung up feeling as if she'd just lost the twenty-pound weight she'd been carrying around on her shoulders. She threw on her jacket and whisked down the street to the cheese shop on Second Avenue.

"WELL, WE CAN'T stand here looking at each other all night," Jenny said to Lynne, breaking the silence that had come over both of them when she'd opened the door several seconds ago. "Come on in."

Lynne held out her package of goodies, which also contained a bottle of wine. "It's not anything near what I owe you, Jenny, but—"

"Let's not talk debits and credits, Lynne," Jenny said kindly, taking the bag from her.

"But I have overdrawn my account with you, Jen, and I'd like to set things right."

"You made a big deposit this afternoon just by calling." Jenny smiled warmly and headed for the kitchen. "Take off your coat and make yourself comfortable. I'll be right back."

Lynne stood still for a moment and then hung her coat on the rack in the foyer. She looked at the arrangement of the furniture before choosing one of the two small armchairs arranged in front of the coffee table facing the couch. In the kitchen a cork popped and Jenny returned with a glass of wine for each of them.

"I feel very awkward," Lynne confessed as she took a glass from Jenny.

"So do I." Jenny settled herself on the edge of the couch.

"You shouldn't," Lynne said strongly. "I'm the one who acted like a spoiled child, who jumped to the wrong conclusions."

"I could have tried harder to make you see you were wrong," Jenny said. She paused and looked at Lynne closely. "But you made me so angry," she added vehemently. "You were so stubborn."

Lynne looked away. She had not only angered her friend, she had hurt her. "I'm sorry, Jenny. Really sorry."

"So am I," Jenny said softly.

There was a long silence between them, the air thick with words that had remained too long unspoken. The few that had come out reverberated in the room, bouncing off the walls and furniture until they finally came to rest.

"I missed you," Lynne said in a small voice. Her words seemed to echo in the room like words sent into a deep canyon.

"You did?" Jenny's response made a smaller softer echo, like words sent down a long hallway. The gap between them was closing.

"Of course I did."

"I missed you, too. After I stopped wanting to box your silly ears."

"I wish you had," Lynne told her, venturing a glimmer of a grin. "It would have saved us all a lot of trouble."

"Who's all?" Jenny asked slyly.

Lynne turned pink with embarrassment. "You know," she said sheepishly. "You, me...Josh."

"Ah, yes. How is our mutual friend?" Jenny emphasized the last word.

"Fine," Lynne answered, a smile sneaking into her lips.

"How fine?"

"Very fine."

"That good?"

"Better."

"It sure took you long enough," Jenny said wryly.

"I really have been a jerk, haven't I?" Lynne made a face of self-exasperation.

"You sure have," Jenny agreed heartily.

"Thanks a lot!"

"But you had a little help from your friends."

"That kind of help I could do without in future. But I hope I won't have to do without my friends. That was tough."

"If I have anything to do with it, you won't have to, Lynne."

"Oh, Jen," Lynne breathed. She put down her wineglass and stood up. Jenny stood and in a wink they were hugging each other and patting each other on the back. "What a mess this all was," Lynne said, blinking back tears.

"A very big mess," Jenny agreed.

They separated and flopped down on the couch side by side.

"So?" Jenny said after a while. "Are you going to keep me in suspense all night?"

"About what?" Lynne asked innocently.

"Don't give me that routine, Farrell, come clean," she demanded.

"He's wonderful," Lynne said.

"I know that. I want the details, all of 'em."

Lynne launched into an account of the past weeks and by the time she was finished half a bottle of wine had disappeared and they were giggling like schoolgirls.

"We'd better eat something or we're going to be totally pie-eyed," Jenny counseled.

Together they set the table and got the meal ready. When they sat down to brimming bowls of fragrant hot soup Lynne said, "Enough about me. I want to know what's going on with you. I'm particularly suspicious about this attack of domesticity. Not like you, Howard." She tasted the soup. "Although I have to say I appreciate the results. This is delicious."

"Thanks." Jenny tasted a spoonful. "Not bad, even if I say so myself."

"Don't change the subject," Lynne admonished.

"Gimme a chance, Lynne," Jenny said a little sharply.

"Sorry." Lynne held up a hand in a truce sign. "Guess I'm still trying a little hard with you." *Hurts and hard feelings don't disappear instantly. They have to be massaged and coaxed away,* she reminded herself.

"That's okay," Jenny consoled with a wave of her fingers. "It'll be a while before we're really comfortable with each other again. Let's just take it easy on each other, okay?"

"Sure," Lynne said.

They ate quietly for a few minutes and then Jenny began to tell the story of meeting a sandy-haired man with glasses in the Strand Book Store one day, and then running into him again when she was with

Josh. "I've seen him several times since then. He's a free-lance journalist, has a loft he refinished himself just a few blocks from here." Jenny described his place, the projects David McGee was working on, the dates they'd had. She and Lynne finished their meal and Jenny still had things to say about him. "He's so smart, Lynne. And not just book smart. He sees things, makes connections."

"He sounds terrific," Lynne said.

"I'd love you and Josh to meet him. Maybe the four of us could get together sometime."

"We'd love that," Lynne enthused. "Or at least, I'd love it. I'll have to check with Josh, of course. See? I've learned my lesson about taking things—and friends—for granted. I've learned a lot in the last couple of months. It wasn't always easy, though."

"I don't think it ever is," Jenny replied. "Or that it's supposed to be."

"No, I guess it isn't," Lynne agreed.

While Jenny made some coffee and warmed up their dessert of pecan tarts, Lynne wandered over to the window. It was a clear night and from the twenty-third floor she was high enough to see a star or two twinkling in the blue velvet city sky. She picked the brightest and, feeling just young enough, just fresh enough to believe in the age-old formula, she uttered a long wish, as she had done so often as a child.

"Did you say something?" Jenny asked, coming into the room.

"Just wishing on that star over there."

"Don't tell me what it was. It won't come true."

"It already has," Lynne said quietly. "That was just for safety's sake."

Jenny hooked her arm through Lynne's and they stood looking at the sky together until the smell of burning pastry sent them both racing into the smoky kitchen.

"Oh, well," Lynne said philosophically, looking down at the blackened mounds on the cookie sheet Jenny was holding in an oven-mitted hand. "We didn't really want dessert, did we? This has already been a pretty sweet evening."

"Don't get mushy on me, Farrell. You'll make me cry."

EPILOGUE

LYNNE SKIPPED MERRILY through the early-spring sunshine, breathing in the clean morning air deeply, feeling inexplicably excited. She chalked it up to the weather: light so clear it made objects seem to be outlined, a musky warmth she could almost taste, the smell of incipient growth lurking just beyond her nose. She bounded into the squash club and nipped down to the locker room. She was into her shorts and T-shirt in no time.

The court was empty when she arrived. *Good,* she thought, *I'll have time to warm up before Josh gets here.* She bounced the ball a few times and started to hit it with sure easy strokes. Everything felt good this morning, none of that waiting for her body to tune up like a car in the cold weather. All systems were go: heart pumping, blood churning, breathing regular but deep, muscles as elastic as rubber bands. She began to hit the ball a little harder, a little faster, but just as surely and easily.

JOSH WAS OUT OF BED before the alarm rang, having awakened spontaneously, as if even in sleep he'd known the morning was so perfect he shouldn't waste a moment of it. He washed and shaved quickly, eager to get to the squash club, eager to play, even more eager to see Lynne. Though he'd spoken to her the night before they hadn't seen each other for a couple of days. And that was entirely too long as far as he was concerned. *I must be getting addicted to that woman,* he thought as he wiped a bit of shaving cream from his chin. But it was an addiction he had no intention of breaking.

He grabbed his gear and walked briskly to the club, nodding along the way to the joggers and dog walkers he passed. For some reason he was feeling extremely friendly this morning. He had an almost irresistible urge to shake the hands of everyone he encountered, to reach down and pet the dogs, even to hug a particularly lovely little old lady. Must be the weather, he decided, noticing how blue the sky was and how there were minute pale green buds barely noticeable to the naked eye peeping from the ends of tree branches.

At the club he changed quickly and bounded up to the court. Through the glass wall he saw Lynne taking a few warm-up shots, looking more lovely than usual, if that was possible. When she saw him there she smiled and his temperature rose a few degrees, as it so often did when she looked at him. He walked onto the court and kissed her playfully on the nose and seriously on the mouth, so seriously that he began to doubt his ability to play a serious game of squash.

Lynne pushed him away reluctantly. "Later for that," she murmured. "We've only got the court for half an hour."

"Just trying to wear down the competition," he said and dived in for one more quick kiss.

"You're not doing a bad job," Lynne whispered, nibbling at his lips. "You're unscrupulous, you know."

"I know." He tore himself away from her and they both took a couple of deep breaths.

Josh spun his racket and won the serve. "Watch out, kid, I feel great this morning. If this was a tennis court I'd have McEnroe on his knees by the end of the first set."

"Ha!" Lynne scoffed. But Josh did look unusually energetic this morning, and even more handsome and desirable. With each passing day he'd become more and more dear to her, but as well as she had come to know him, as close as she felt to him, as much as she loved him, every time she saw him she was astounded at how good he looked to her and how strong her feelings for him were. "Skip the psychology. Just get going."

They played full out from the first service, a rousing rollicking game, hitting as many barbs back and forth as balls. It was a close game, too, with the lead bouncing back and forth like a rubber ball. Lynne knew their thirty minutes were more than half over and she pressed an attack to move ahead, but every time she did Josh caught up with her.

After winning a hard point from him to regain service and keep the score tied, she thought she had the edge and slammed a tricky serve in the hopes of acing him. But he returned the ball and they started a long volley, both of them hitting and returning some of the most brilliant and impossible shots ever. Lynne had just hit what she thought was a sure winner when Josh suddenly fell to his knees in the middle of the court and collapsed in a heap on the floor.

She raced frantically to his side. "Are you hurt?" He didn't answer. "Josh!" she was fairly shaking with fright as she dropped to her knees beside him. "Are you all right?"

Slowly he raised his head. "I love you," he said quietly.

"What?" She grabbed at his wrist to take his pulse.

"I love you, and I want you to marry me."

"You want to marry me? You scared me half to death, Josh. I thought you'd had a heart attack."

"I did," he said with a silly grin. "All of a sudden I loved you so much I couldn't stand it another minute. I had to ask you to marry me. I love you, Lynnie." He put his arms around her and kissed her so ardently Lynne was sure that if she opened her eyes there would be steam rising on the court. "So what's your answer?" he asked, releasing her only far enough to allow himself to speak.

"I'd like some time to think about it," she replied. She knew what her answer was but she wanted him to sweat for a minute. He deserved it for scaring her half out of her wits.

He looked crestfallen. "What's there to think about?"

"Honestly, Josh, we're in the middle of a squash court. We're in the middle of a point. How do you expect me to answer such an important question at a time like this?"

"You're kidding," he said.

She put on her sternest look—with much difficulty—and said, "No, I'm not. We've got just enough time to finish this point. I'll tell you after the game is over." She stood up.

"Give a guy a break. I just asked you to marry me."

"Play, Josh."

He scrambled to his feet and took up his racket. "Okay. If that's the way you want it."

She served the point and Josh sent the ball at her so fast she hardly saw it coming. But she caught it and slammed it back. He ran her all over the court, this way and that, dropping shots where he thought she couldn't possibly get them and groaning heavily when she did. Lynne was tempted a number of times to give up, to lay down her racket and say yes, yes, yes, yes, yes. But it wasn't good to start a marriage on an unequal footing. She didn't care who won the point, just that they played it out to the end—honestly and with as much skill and intelligence as they could bring to bear. Exactly as she hoped they'd live the rest of their lives together.

For a split second her concentration wavered and Josh found his opening. He hit home a shot that she couldn't get, though she tried valiantly for it. He threw down his racket and ran toward her. "What's your answer?" he cried.

"There's only one possible answer, Josh," she said nonchalantly. "Yes. I don't see what you're getting so excited about."

"You will in a minute," he said huskily.

He took her in his arms and kissed her deeply, pulling her in closer and closer to him until Lynne was unsure where he left off and she started. "I've never seen anyone so happy to have won a point," she whispered, breaking way from him for a moment.

"That had nothing to do with it, and you know

it." He pulled her closer again and continued their kiss. From somewhere in the distance she heard the court bell sound and doors opening and closing. But the noises had nothing to do with her. She was being kissed by her husband-to-be. He tasted salty and tangy like the sea, and she had as much love for him as there were drops of water in the ocean.

There was a sharp knocking, but she ignored it. They both ignored it until there was a loud cough and an amused voice said, "Excuse me. I don't want to break in, but your time's up."

Josh surfaced and gave the man a broad smile. "No, it's just beginning."

"There must be some mistake. My partner and I—" He indicated another man behind him.

Josh and Lynne both burst out laughing. "That's not what he meant," Lynne explained. "Excuse us," she said, pulling Josh off the court.

"Yes, I did," Josh protested as he shut the court door behind them. He pulled Lynne to him again. "We're just starting, Lynnie. We've got a whole long wonderful life ahead of us."

"I know, Josh."

"Will you promise me something?"

"I've just promised you everything," she whispered. "What else can I give you, my love?"

"I just want to be sure, Lynnie, that when you start being my wife you won't stop being my friend, my best friend."

"I'll always be your friend first, Josh. And your lover and," she said solemnly, "your wife."

"And you're going to stop beating me at squash," he said matter-of-factly.

Lynne pushed herself away from him and placed

her hands squarely on her hips. "If you think that, buddy..." she began.

"Just joking," he said with a playful smile, squashing the rest of her protest with a heart-stopping, life-starting kiss.

Harlequin Announces...
Harlequin Superromance™
NEW
IMPROVED EXCELLENCE

Beginning with February releases (titles #150 to #153) each of the four Harlequin Superromances will be 308 pages long and have a regular retail price of $2.75 ($2.95 in Canada).

The new shortened Harlequin Superromance guarantees a faster-paced story filled with the same emotional intensity, character depth and plot complexity you have come to expect from Harlequin Superromance.

The tighter format will heighten drama and excitement, and that, combined with a strong well-written romance, will allow you to become more involved with the story from start to finish.

Available wherever paperback books are sold or through Harlequin Reader Service:

In the U.S.
P.O. Box 52040
Phoenix, AZ 85072-2040

In Canada
P.O. Box 2800, Postal Station A
5170 Yonge Street
Willowdale, Ontario M2N 6J3

Share the joys and sorrows of real-life love with
Harlequin American Romance!™

GET THIS BOOK FREE
as your introduction to Harlequin American Romance — an exciting series of romance novels written especially for the American woman of today.

Mail to:
Harlequin Reader Service

In the U.S.
2504 West Southern Ave.
Tempe, AZ 85282

In Canada
P.O. Box 2800, Postal Station A
5170 Yonge St., Willowdale, Ont. M2N 5T5

YES! I want to be one of the first to discover **Harlequin American Romance**. Send me FREE and without obligation *Twice in a Lifetime*. If you do not hear from me after I have examined my FREE book, please send me the 4 new **Harlequin American Romances** each month as soon as they come off the presses. I understand that I will be billed only $2.25 for each book (total $9.00). There are no shipping or handling charges. There is no minimum number of books that I have to purchase. In fact, I may cancel this arrangement at any time. *Twice in a Lifetime* is mine to keep as a FREE gift, even if I do not buy any additional books.

Name	(please print)	
Address		Apt. no.
City	State/Prov.	Zip/Postal Code

Signature (If under 18, parent or guardian must sign.)

This offer is limited to one order per household and not valid to current Harlequin American Romance subscribers. We reserve the right to exercise discretion in granting membership. If price changes are necessary, you will be notified.

AMR-SUB-1

154-BPA-NAZJ